CROSSROADS MURDER

Crossroads Murder

Clyde Skaggs

Clyde Skaggs

Minuteman Press
Liverpool, New York

PUBLISHED BY CWS ENTERPRISES
4023 Brixham Ct., Baldwinsville, NY 13027

This is a work of fiction. The characters are products of the author's imagination and are not to be construed as real. Any resemblance to actual persons, living or dead, is entirely coincidental. All places and events are fictitious, or are used in a fictional manner.

Cover design, cover photographs and Book design by Clyde Skaggs.
4023 Brixham Court
Baldwinsville, NY 13027

ISBN 0-9743003-0-6

Manufactured in the United States of America
August 2003

FOR JESSIE

Acknowledgements

Thanks to my wife for her patience and understanding.

CROSSROADS MURDER

CHAPTER ONE

(Tuesday Night)

It was a beautiful day in central New York and Backus Gibbs spent the day at his job cutting grass for the Sunset Pine golf course. He finished work at six o'clock, changed his shoes at work as usual, and went home.

He showered, dried quickly, and parted his black hair in the middle. He ran the razor over his square jaw and put on washed out jeans and a blue, plaid, shirt. Backus was 31 years old, five foot ten inches tall, and weighed a hundred fifty pounds.

He left the house at six thirty, stopped and had pizza for dinner and was now headed to do a special and different kind of job. It was starting to get dark at about 7:30 p.m. when Backus drove his nineteen eighty-eight gray Ford into the underground parking lot of the Crossroads Mall. He pulled into a parking space not far from one of the glass door entrances leading into the lower level of the mall. After parking, he stayed in the car smoking a cigarette and staring into space.

Four weeks earlier, Gibbs, had gone to Sidney Drango's office to borrow money for gambling at the racetrack. When Gibbs opened the office door, the short fat loan shark was leaning over his desk dressed in wrinkled, baggy, blue pants, a black turtleneck shirt that was too tight around his pot-belly and a light blue-checkered sport coat that he couldn't button. As Gibbs entered, Drango looked up over the top of his glasses that had slid down on his nose and said, "What the hell do you want?"

"I need to borrow some more money."

"Bullshit, you owe me a fortune already and you aren't even keeping up with the interest."

"I know, but I got a hot tip at Vernon Downs and if you give me this loan, I'll be able to score big, and then pay you what I owe."

Every weekend since he came to Syracuse, Gibbs had been visiting the off-track betting office, the harness racing track or, the Indian casino, and some weekends, more than one. He tried to limit his losses to a hundred dollars at a time but wasn't always successful. Occasionally he would win a little, usually just enough to keep him coming back. Over most of the five years, he had been borrowing from Drango and had run up a debt that he would never be able to repay unless he could win big.

"Yeah, right, I've heard that before," Drango said.

"If you don't give me another loan, I don't know how I'll ever settle my debt. I'm already giving you most of my pay every week and the debt keeps growing because of the interest."

"You should've thought of that before you borrowed the money, stupid. And now you want to borrow more. You dumb shit! There's only one way you'll ever settle your debt, and that's by doing a special job for me."

Gibbs had done jobs for Drango before, mostly strong-arm stuff to help him collect money. The pay had always been pretty good.

"What's the job and how much does it pay?" Gibbs asked, wide eyed.

"I want someone killed."

"I've never killed anyone," he exclaimed nervously.

"If you do this thing for me, I'll erase your debt."

"The whole twenty five thousand?" Gibbs asked incredulously.

"That's right."

"Who do you want killed?"

"Roger Moreland."

"The mayor? Are you serious?"

"Dead serious."

"When would I have to do it?" he asked shifting back and forth from one foot to the other.

"That's up to you, but the sooner, the better"

"Jesus Sid, this is a serious thing you're asking me to do. I gotta think about it."

"Well, don't take too long stupid, or I just might take your ass instead. Now get out, and let me hear from you soon. I'm making you a very generous offer, and it won't be on the table very long."

"Okay," Gibbs muttered, "I'll think about it and get

back to you right away Sid." He turned toward the door and left more distressed than he'd been when he came in. Drango knew he had him hooked.

It had been four weeks since that meeting with Drango and Gibbs had been following the mayor for three of them. Most of the time, the mayor was chauffeured around in a city car. On the previous two Tuesdays, however, the mayor used his own car and came to the mall alone. On both occasions, he went into the mall by the same door, stayed for an hour and a half, and came out alone and left. Gibbs assumed that he would do the same thing tonight, so he came early to watch and wait. As he expected, Moreland drove into the parking lot a little before eight and parked in the same general area he had on the two previous occasions. Gibbs lit another cigarette and waited. The mall door that the mayor used had a security camera mounted in the ceiling that viewed people leaving and entering the door. The good news for Gibbs was that the camera only looked at the door. He had determined that fact with what he thought was a great deal of cleverness. He had leaned a stick against the wall at the corner next to the door, first on the right side and then later, on the left side of the door and on both occasions, had laid a piece of paper on the ground in front of the door. Then he walked past the open security office a number of times looking at the monitors. After several passes, he located the screen showing the door with the paper in front. Furtively then, he observed the camera could not see the concrete block wall where he had stood the stick on the two occasions. He then knew that if he stayed past the corner on either the right or left hand side of the door the camera would not see him.

As ten p.m. and closing of the mall approached, the number of people coming out decreased, and along with them, so had the number of cars leaving the parking lot.

Gibbs had given a lot of thought to how he would do the job before he called Drango and agreed to it. He would use his blackjack to knock the mayor out before he had a chance to make a noise or put up a struggle. Then he would pull him back, lay him down, and stab him to death. That way he wouldn't get any blood on his clothes. Then, as an extra measure, Gibbs decided that he would take the mayor's watch and money to make it look like a robbery.

Gibbs, sweating as he sat in the car, went over the details again in his mind. He had attached the light brown leather sheath containing his fishing knife to his belt so his jacket hid it, yet it was easy to get. The wooden handled knife had a seven-inch blade he kept very sharp and the back edge of it was serrated along three inches for scaling fish. Gibbs liked to fish, but always threw them back. He had cleaned fish only once and thought it too messy. He planned the murder so it wouldn't be messy and he wouldn't get any blood on himself. The blackjack he would use to knock the mayor out with was important to his plan. He would keep it in his right hand in his pants pocket so when the time came, he would be ready.

At 9:10 Gibbs put out his cigarette, and immediately lit another. He opened the car door, and got out. His heart was beating so fast, he was afraid he might faint. He walked towards the mall entrance and turned right just before getting there to make sure he'd stay out of the view of the camera. He leaned against the wall nervously taking quick puffs on his cigarette while he waited and looked at his watch frequently. At precisely 9:15, he threw the cigarette down, walked up near the corner by the door, and waited. At 9:20, the mayor came through the door and started for the parking lot.

Gibbs recognized him from behind by the white hair, the blue plaid sports coat, and gray slacks. As soon as the mayor was out of camera range, Gibbs quickly moved forward, his heart racing even faster, and put his left arm around the man's neck. Then, as quickly and as hard as he could, he hit him on the head with the blackjack. The mayor never knew what hit him. Gibbs then dragged him back along the wall and laid him down on his back. He pulled his arms straight out over his head so that his body would lay closer to the wall and rolled him over face down. Trembling, he pulled out the knife and repeatedly stabbed his victim in the back. Almost gagging from the smell caused by relaxation and emptying of the mayor's bowels and bladder, he inflicted the last thrust, then looked around carefully.

Although there was still a number of cars in the garage, he saw only one person and she was far away coming out of one of the store elevators exiting into the parking lot. She was walking towards her car with her back towards him. He wiped the knife blade on the dead man's back and put it in its sheath.

Afterward, he pulled the mayor's gold watch from his wrist and lifted the tail of the man's sport coat looking for the bulge of his wallet. The thick leather billfold had a large number of bills in it, and he put them along with the watch in his pocket. The mayor's coattail was used to wipe his fingerprints from the wallet. He then dropped it alongside the body in the corner.

The deed done, Gibbs stood and looked around again to make sure nobody was watching, before finally heading for his car. It was exactly 9:35 when he went through the garage door exiting the parking lot onto Loop Road. Leaving the mall property, he headed towards downtown and the safety of his apartment.

CHAPTER TWO

(Later Tuesday Night)
  Detective Jonathan J. Broder had gone to bed early Tuesday night and was sound asleep when the phone rang at twelve thirty. He rolled over, propped himself up on one elbow and grabbed it before it could ring a second time. In a sleepy voice, he said, "Hello".
  " Jon, this is Captain Sheppard."
  "Yeah?" He muttered, still half asleep, "What's up?"
  "There's been a murder at the Crossroads Mall in the underground parking lot. Can you get down there right away?"
  "Sure," as if he had a choice, he thought, "as soon as I can get dressed. It'll take me half an hour to get there."
  "Jon, you better hurry."
  "Yeah? Why?" he asked, sitting up straight and rubbing his eyes with the knuckle of his left hand.

"It looks like the victim is the mayor."

"Oh shit, you mean our mayor, Roger Moreland? He thought his sleepiness had caused him to hear wrong."

"That's right," Sheppard said, "when I got the call they hadn't turned the body over yet, so they couldn't see the face, but there was an open wallet beside the body with the mayor's driver's license in it. I'd say it's pretty certain to be him. When you get there have someone call me and confirm so I can inform his family."

"What happened . . ." he started to ask, and then said, "Oh forget it, I'll hurry" and he started to hang up without bothering to say good-by when the captain said, "Jon, be in front of the headquarters building at eight o'clock this morning for a news conference. The chief has prepared a short statement and won't take any questions. I'll see you then and we'll have a meeting in my office at 10:30, following the conference, good bye"

Jon Broder was forty-five and had been a cop for twenty-five years. He was an optimist by nature, believed in the American dream, motherhood, and his partner, not necessarily in that order. He tried to do things right, be honest, and not criticize, condemn or complain. Obviously, he didn't always succeed, but he kept trying. He truly believed that if you couldn't say something nice about a person, you shouldn't say anything. This philosophy, of course, didn't apply to all aspects of his work. He thought everything should have a place and everything should be in its place. The last fifteen years had been spent in homicide. His premature gray hair had started out as a few hairs at the age of eighteen and gradually grown over the years to leave his present full head of grayish white hair. He had an angular face and was in good shape. He played golf and tennis when he had time, and walked at least three times a week.

As Jon reached into the closet for his jacket, he noticed the last sweater his ex-wife Annie had bought for him. It was thirteen years ago that he had been working very hard to make lieutenant and was feeling pretty good about the job when he came home one night after midnight from a tough case and Annie said, "Jon, this is ridiculous. You're never home except to sleep and on a rare occasion eat. We do nothing together and have no friends. All we do is live in the same house and sleep together, in a loveless, sexless marriage. Frankly, I can't take it any more. I want out!"

"Annie . . ." he started to say in a pleading voice.

"Don't Annie me," she said, "we've had this discussion before and nothing ever changes. I've already talked to a lawyer and the papers will be ready Friday. Now you can sleep on the couch tonight, but tomorrow, I want you out of the house."

Christ, seven years of marriage down the drain, he'd thought, but there was no talking her out of it. The sad part of it was, he loved her very much. Looking back on it he realized she'd been right. His job at that time didn't leave room for anything else. So that's how it had ended. Three months later the divorce was complete and they had gone their separate ways. She had gotten the house, the furniture and the '95 Chevy. He had gotten the '93 S-10 pickup, his chair, and Maggie their tiger kitten.

Annie subsequently sold the three-bedroom two story colonial house to get the equity, which pleased Jonathan, since he no longer had to make the mortgage payments.

Fortunately, there were no children. They wanted to have a baby, but each time they discussed when, it seemed that they couldn't quite afford it and decided to wait.

Since the divorce, Jon lived in a small two-bedroom apartment in a planned community development on the northwest side of town where there was a golf course, swimming pool, tennis courts, and walking trails. He had transformed his life into one of quiet comfort, and mild physical recreation, taking advantage of the amenities offered by the development. One thing hadn't changed much, though; he still worked wild and long hours under a great deal of stress. What had changed was the fact that he now kept the job in proper perspective and didn't let it become all- consuming.

Before leaving the house, Jon called his partner Micheal Crane, got him out of bed and asked him to meet him at the mall-parking garage.

Micheal was six feet, weighed one hundred eighty pounds and was about ten years younger than Jon. Mike was married with one son and thought much the same way as Jon. They were very considerate and compatible partners. Mike jumped out of bed, ran a comb through his brown hair, stretched to his full six-foot height and put on his glasses. He didn't even bother to wash the sleep out of his eyes. He grabbed a pair of jeans and blue golf shirt laying on the back of a chair, pulled them on, kissed his wife Martha on the forehead, and took off for the mall.

When Jonathan arrived at the scene there was a blockade at the underground parking garage doors. Once he showed his credentials and was allowed through, he saw that the crime-scene-unit truck and the medical examiner's station wagon were already there along with three police cars with their lights flashing. Jon surveyed the area and could see that one of the entrances to the lower level of the mall had been cordoned off by yellow tape. In accordance with protocol, the tape had been stretched around the scene to prevent accidental contamination of evidence. Using the large concrete pillars supporting the upper floors of the mall, they had marked off one bay, which was approximately twenty-four feet square. It was also dark, damp, and musty with most of the pavement covered with oil and grease. The incandescent lights on the ceiling did little to expel the gloomy appearance of the unpainted concrete ceiling, pillars, and floor.

As Micheal parked his Honda near Jonathan's truck, he noticed his partner had just started over towards the medical examiner, who was kneeling over the body. Micheal caught up to Jonathan and they walked over where they could get a good look at the body. Micheal asked the police officer standing at the edge of the small crowd around the yellow tape who was controlling the scene.

"Pete Brady, my partner," the officer said, as he pointed his thumb toward another police officer standing farther down the line.

The medical examiner was studying the body and a crime scene photographer was taking pictures. The victim was laying face down against the corner where the wall meets the floor with both arms stretched over his head. Broder asked the ME if the body had been moved. He said, "No. I was waiting for you to get here. There's a wallet lying wide open on the pavement and we're guessing it belongs to the victim by its position in relation to the body. I didn't touch it, but as soon as you look at it, you'll see the mayor's face on his driver's license."

Jon walked around the crime scene and noticed a camera on the ceiling pointing at the door. He saw a tall thin security guard with gray hair standing near the door and asked him if the camera worked.

"Yes," he said. We reviewed the film but it didn't show anything except the mayor coming out the door.

"Why didn't it show anything if it was working?" Jon asked.

The camera has a very narrow field of view and is a stationary camera, which only sees the door. I don't know why the camera doesn't scan unless it was a cost consideration at the time of installation of the system. Normally a camera of that type with a narrow field of view is used for a scanning installation. Maybe someone made a mistake when they installed it and used the wrong camera. Anyway, I made a copy of the film thinking that you'd want it."

"You're right, I do. Thank you. Would you mind getting it for me now so I won't forget?"

"No problem," he said. "It's in the office and it'll only take me a few minutes to get it."

"While Jon was making notes in his notebook about the camera, the security guard came back and handed him the VHS tape which Jon slipped into the side pocket of his sport coat.

Pete Brady who was about five foot eight and had a small frame was having a hard time keeping the dozen or so people back away from the tape. Three other policemen in blue uniforms were assisting him.

"Officer Brady?" Micheal asked.

"Yes? I'm Brady."

Micheal flashed his shield and said, "I'm Detective Crane, homicide and that's my partner Lieutenant Broder. Is there anything besides what you might've told the ME that I should know?"

"Well," Brady said, "my partner and I were finishing up our shift and heading for downtown. It was about ten o'clock when the call came through saying there was a problem here in the parking garage. Since we were an exit away on the interstate, we decided to answer the call. When we arrived the security guard met us at the overhead doors and led us to the body. As far as I know, we, the guy who found the body and the guard, were the first on the scene."

"Who found the body?"

"A Mr. Tomson. He came out that door, went to his car, that green Ford over there, and as he was unlocking it,

14

looked up and saw the body laying back here on the ground at the base of the wall. He didn't see it when he came out the door because it was around the corner. I guess that's why no one else saw it either. You just had to be looking in the right direction. Anyway, when he saw blood, he ran back inside to call 911, and ran into a security guard who helped him. He didn't even check the body."

"Where is the witness?" Crane asked.

"Over there in the squad car," Brady said. "I took his statement, but he didn't say much more than what I just told you. Did you hear who . . .?" Brady started to ask, nodding back over his shoulder.

"Yeah, I heard," Mike said. He turned and then walked to the squad car.

"How are you sir"? Mike said to the witness when he reached the squad car. The man of about thirty-five, with blond hair and glasses had been staring into space and was startled when Mike spoke to him. "I'm Detective Crane, homicide. What's your name?"

"George Tomson", the man replied.

"Can you tell me what you saw, Mr. Tomson?"

The man was nervous and replied, "I already told the officers."

"I know," Crane conceded, "but I'd like to hear it again if you don't mind."

"Well, I came out that door," he pointed to the glass door leading into the lower level of the mall. "And went over to my car. As I was unlocking it, I glanced up and saw the body around the corner." He pointed in the direction of the door. "At first, I wondered if someone had a heart attack, but as I approached the body, I saw there was a lot of blood. That's when I ran inside to call 911 and ran into the security guard who helped me."

"What time was that?" Mike asked.

"About a quarter to ten," he said.

"What were you doing here so late?"

"I was at a writer's group meeting in Binder's Bookstore on the other side of the mall. I knew the mall parking garage closes at eleven so I left the meeting early to make sure I didn't get locked in. The meeting goes until eleven." He added.

"Were you by yourself coming from the meeting?"

"Yes, I came to the meeting alone and this was the first meeting I've attended so I didn't know I should have parked outside the bookstore on the other side of the mall. The rest of the group was still there when I left."

"Okay, tell me, did you know who the victim was?" Mike asked.

"No sir, I didn't look at the body."

"Did you see anyone else in the parking lot?"

"There were two or three people getting into their cars, but the mall was about empty. Most of the stores close at ten."

"Was there anyone else nearby when you discovered the body?"

"No sir."

"Okay", Mike said, "you can go back to your car, but it'll be a little while before you can leave because of the barricades. We may contact you again and may ask you to come to headquarters. Did you give the other officer your phone number and address?"

"Yes I did," he said, getting out of the police car. He walked off towards his car.

Micheal walked over to where Jon and Brady were standing near the body, which had been turned over by the ME. As they suspected it was, in fact, the mayor. He said to Brady, "did anyone touch the body before the CSU and the ME arrived?"

"No sir, I radioed dispatch a few minutes after ten and asked that the ME and CSU be sent out and they arrived at 10:25. When we saw the wallet with the mayor's picture, I radioed dispatch back and told them. They said that they'd call the captain."

"Good," Broder said. "Oh, by the way, call the captain and confirm identification of the body so he can go see the mayor's wife and give her the bad news."

The small crowd of people around the yellow tape wasn't getting any bigger. The police had blocked off the four entrance doors to the parking lot and were not letting any more vehicles enter or leave.

Jonathan told Brady to get his partner and move the people back and double check to see if anyone else had seen or heard anything. If they did he wanted to talk to them. He also told Brady that he wanted him personally to clear every car before it left the garage to make sure every one in the area had been interviewed.

Jon turned and knelt down along side the medical examiner, Dr. Mark Towsen. He was a man about 60 with white hair, wire glasses and about 50 extra pounds around his middle. Broder shook hands with him, and said, "What have we got Doc?"

"Well", Towsen said, using the knuckle of his gloved right hand to push his glasses up against his sweaty nose, "he's been stabbed six times in the back, and from the rigor mortis, I'd say he's been dead three to five hours. There's also a bruise on his throat. It might suggest he was grabbed from behind. The big contusion on his head here also supports that theory. "I can't tell what kind of knife until I perform the autopsy. It doesn't look like there was much of a struggle. I think he was surprised."

"Anything else?"

"Not until I cut him open," Towsen said.

"Doc, tell me. I'm thinking the way his arms are stretched over his head; he might've been dragged over here.

"I'd say it's possible but unlikely because there is no blood trail. It's more likely he was held up and pulled back, which would account for absence of blood except where he's laying. It's also unlikely he was killed someplace else and dumped here. If that were so, the amount of blood around the body, would be a great deal less. My guess is the killer grabbed him from behind as he came out of the door; like this - he put his left arm around Jon's neck to demonstrate - hit him on the head with a blunt instrument and held him up dragging him, while upright, back out of sight. If you look there," he pointed to the pavement, "you can see what looks like heel marks. I think he was stabbed after he was dragged back out of sight and laid down. Then the arms stretched out that way so that the body would lay closer to the wall and not be so visible."

"Now that you point it out," Broder said, "that makes a lot of sense. Thanks, Doc. I'll bring somebody in tomorrow to make a formal identification."

Broder turned and headed for one of the Crime Scene Technicians. He was about thirty years old, with dark hair and was very thin and wore a white lab coat. Jon didn't recognize him.

"Hi, I'm Detective Lieutenant Jonathan Broder, homicide, and you are?"

"Tom Wilder, "I've been with the lab for about two months

'Tom, do you know who the victim is?"

"Yes sir, I do."

"This is going to be a very high profile case, so make sure you do it by the book. Got it? Everything! If there is anything you're not absolutely sure about, you ask!"

"Yes sir," Wilder said.

"Okay, I'll let you finish your work now." But as he left him, Jonathan looked over his shoulder and asked Wilder one final question. "When can I expect a report?"

"A couple of days," hc said.

"Do it right, but get it to me as fast as you can."

Jon walked over to Brady. "Can you clear the people away with the help you've got or do you need more assistance?"

"No sir, my partner Pat and I with help from the other three officers can handle it just fine."

"Broder said, "Be sure and get their names, addresses, and telephone numbers before you let them go."

"Yes sir."

Jonathan walked up to Mike and said, "Lets go to our office, make some coffee and sort things out."

"Right, I'll meet you there in ten minutes," Mike said, heading for his car.

In the office, Jon said, "Aren't we the lucky ones?"

"Yeah," Mike said. "What do you suppose happened?"

"It appears that the mayor came out the door and someone was waiting around the corner for him." Jon related to Mike the theory that Doc Towsen had put forth.

"Makes sense." Mike said. "Robbery could be a motive since his money and watch were missing, assuming that he had money in his wallet, and that he wore a watch."

Jon pulled the tape out of his coat pocket and laid it on the desk. The security guy at the mall gave me this. Said it showed the mayor coming through the door, but nothing else because of its narrow field of view. We'll look it over a little later.

"When I talked to the captain, he told me the chief's calling a press conference at eight this morning; downstairs in front of the building and he wants us there. We don't have to say anything. The chief's going to read a short statement and won't take any questions. It's almost five now and I'm really beat. Let's go home, get a couple of hours shuteye, and then meet back here in time for the news conference. Hopefully by then we'll be bright eyed and bushy tailed and can plan our strategy after the conference."

"Sounds good," Mike said, draining his coffee and getting up. " I'll see you in a little while. He left with Jonathan right behind him.

When Jon walked into his apartment and turned on the light. Maggie was sitting in the middle of the living room. He'd gotten Maggie as a kitten shortly before the divorce. Maggie was getting old now at thirteen and they were great friends. The silky sheen of her coat was due to the fact that Jon brushed her often; something that she seemed to enjoy very much.

"What's the matter Maggie, can't sleep?" She meowed walking slowly towards him.

"I'll bet your hungry," he said. "C'mon, it's almost time for your breakfast." He went to the kitchen with the cat on his heels and opened a can of Friskies Beef and Liver, one of Maggie's favorites. "There you go," he said, setting the dish on the floor. Then he put on a pot of coffee and retired to his chair in the living room. The brown Barcalounger leather recliner with its worn arms and torn footrest was the only piece of furniture he'd taken from the house after the divorce. It was like an old shoe. In addition to the recliner, the living room had a couch that made a bed, though with two bedrooms, it was never used as a bed, a glass topped coffee table, an occasional chair, and bridge-lamp. A magazine rack table-lamp stood beside his recliner. The living room floor was covered with a bright imitation oriental rug he felt made the place a little more cheery. He sat down in his chair to think about what they had to do tomorrow and before long, fell asleep.

When he woke up it was daylight and the sun was just starting to shine through the trees and into his living room window. It was going to be another beautiful day in Central New York. Maggie, as usual, was asleep on his lap. He rubbed his eyes, scratched Maggie's ears, pushed her off of his lap and went to the kitchen to get a cup of coffee, which by now had been sitting for over an hour and would taste lousy. It was six thirty, which meant he'd have time for an English muffin and coffee before he showered to go to work.

Mike got home from the office at 5:30 a.m. When he went into the bedroom and around to his side of the bed, Martha rolled over, and said, "It's okay, you can turn the light on, I'm awake. What was the call about?"

"I'll tell you in the morning," he said, setting the alarm. He pulled his clothes off, then slid into bed managing to give Martha a kiss just before he fell asleep in her arms.

CHAPTER THREE

(Wednesday)

The alarm went off and Mike covered his head with the pillow. Martha climbed out of bed, slipped on a duster, and tiptoed out of the bedroom. After making a pot of coffee, she went out to the mailbox to get the paper and couldn't believe her eyes when she read the headlines.
'MAYOR MORELAND MURDERED'
In shock, she couldn't help thinking that this was the first day in months that the president hadn't made the front page headlines concerning his alleged sexual misconduct with a young White House intern. Taking a cup of coffee to the bedroom, she sat on the bed, bent over, and gave Mike a kiss on the lips. Coming awake, he returned her kiss.

Pulling her head back, looking at him, and holding the cup where he could see it, she said, "Want some coffee?"

"Does the Pope pray?" he asked, taking the proffered cup. Leaning against the headboard before he took a sip of the coffee and seeing the newspaper in her hands, he said, "The mayor was killed last night, is it in the paper?"

"Sure is," she said, handing him the paper.

"It's amazing how fast they get information," he commented, spreading the paper out on his lap so he could read the headline. "That's where I was last night, turn on the TV."

". . . And the only information available at this point," Jessica Mathews was saying, "came to us from a shopper who happened to be in the Crossroads Mall parking garage near closing time last night. We were told that some time before ten o'clock last night, the mayor, was slain in the underground parking lot of the Crossroads Mall. As yet we have been unable to confirm this information through official channels, but have been informed this morning the chief of police will hold a press conference at eight in front of the Public Safety Building. We assume he'll address this matter then. Stay tuned to TV 2 for live coverage. This is Jessica Mathews reporting live for TV 2 from the Public Safety Building. Now back to our Studio."

Martha turned the TV off.

"I can't believe it Mike, what happened?" she asked in a cracked voice sounding like she might cry."

"You heard," he said. "Some guy coming out of the mall just before ten, saw the body, and phoned it in. Jon called me around 12:30 and we went right down, but the

24

scene didn't hold a lot of promise. I'm going in at eight for the conference. We're supposed to have a crime scene report sometime tomorrow. Perhaps that'll give us a lead," he said, getting out of bed. How about fixing some breakfast while I take a quick shower?"

Martha gave him a quick kiss and headed for the kitchen. Mike smiled to himself watching and admiring his wife of ten years as she left the room, her blond curls bouncing as she went. The kitchen was in the back of the small eight year old cedar-sided ranch style house and as she looked through the Venetian blinds, and out the casement window, she saw two squirrels chasing each other up a tree. They were starting to collect nuts in earnest for the coming winter. After the squirrels were gone from sight, she turned to the stove to fix scrambled eggs. She had just set the plates on the table and was buttering toast when Mike briskly entered the kitchen dressed in tan slacks, a white dress shirt, pale green tie and a brown plaid sport coat.

Pouring himself a cup of coffee, Mike sat down and looked at the paper. While he ate and read, Martha thought about what she had to do; get Jimmy off to school, do the laundry, and go to the grocery store. Since it looked like an easy day, she reasoned that she might schedule events so that she could have lunch out. Finishing his eggs, Mike laid the paper down, and glanced at his watch. Then he kissed Martha good-by, and went out to head for work. Watching him back out of the driveway, Martha sighed and then turned to go check on their eight-year-old son, Jimmy. He was awake lying in bed looking at a book. Martha entered the room saying, "Good morning sleepy head," as she ruffled his blond curly hair.

Smiling in his normal good-natured way, Jimmy said, "Good morning, Mommy."

"Ready for breakfast? What would you like, Cheerios?"

"Okay, and a cinnamon bagel, I'm starved."

"C'mon," she said, heading out of the room. Jimmy threw the covers back, jumped out of bed and hurriedly caught up to his mother and held her hand on the way back to the kitchen.

The Sunset Pine golf course was located about twenty miles northwest of the city and could be reached within a half hour from most anywhere in the area. It was a public course, which sold memberships and was a favorite of Jonathan and Micheal's.

The course was owned by an elderly couple who was past retirement but still enjoyed working at the course every day. They had made the course one of the best-groomed courses in the area. They personally ran the clubhouse, which consisted of a small pro shop and restaurant, but employed a greens keeper who was responsible for seeing that the course was maintained to their specifications. In addition to the greens keeper they employed a retired golf pro to offer lessons to customers. He also passed judgment on and had to approve the people hired by the greens keeper. When the greens keeper hired Backus Gibbs the Pro and the owner agreed with reluctance. The Pro had said, "He doesn't look like a reliable person, he doesn't look very well groomed and he doesn't have any references for this kind of work". The greens keeper had said, "You don't have to socialize with him, I'm just going to use him to cut the grass." That had been five years ago, and as unsavory as Gibbs looked, he had worked out pretty well. He hardly ever missed work and he did an acceptable job cutting the grass. It wasn't easy to get and keep people to cut grass, nor was it a very glamorous job since it didn't pay much.

To Backus the grass cutting job was great. He didn't have to know very much and he didn't have to deal with people. Earlier in the spring, however, he found out that the job could be dangerous. He had been cutting with one of the gang mowers and was on a hill. He was leaning towards the bank as he went along to keep the tractor from tipping when his foot slipped and almost got caught in the mower reel. Fortunately his shoe came off and the mower missed his foot. His shoe, however, had a crescent piece of rubber cut from the sole. He was still able to wear the shoe and, since the incident, he had been more careful.

On the golf course, people were enjoying the sunny blue sky with cumulus clouds near the horizon and the pleasant temperature in the upper seventies. Gibbs, cutting the grass, however, was very nervous since the murder last night and was worrying about the possibility of getting caught. He had decided after the murder he should do his job, lay low, watch the news and try not to worry. But he found today he couldn't stop worrying. His boss told him this would be the last time he'd have to cut the grass since it was November first, even though the course would stay open as long as the weather remained nice. Some people didn't like the weather in Central New York because of the harsh winters; one hundred twenty inches of seasonal snow was normal. But to others, it was a lot better than forest fires, mudslides, hurricanes, and tornadoes. Besides, the DOT in Central New York really knew how to handle snow. Gibbs definitely fit the latter group

When he finished work today, he would call Drango and go pick up his IOUs. With his debt to Drango erased and the pay he would get from the golf course today, he should be able to afford to go away. Maybe he'd go see his mother.

Jonathan was already in the office when Mike arrived at 7:45. He was sitting sideways at his desk. The office was about ten feet by twelve feet and had two desks, two file cabinets, a small conference table and a large square white board on the wall between the two desks. The computer was on a small desk in the corner most remote from the desks. Neither Mike nor Jon used the computer a lot. On one of the file cabinets was a coffee pot. They had an agreement the first person in each morning would put the coffee on.

"Good morning Jon", Mike called, walking into the office.

Jon returned his greeting and said, "The captain wants to see us in his office at 10:30, so we'll have to get our thoughts sorted out right after the news conference. Now, we better get downstairs because it's ten till eight."

Half of the street in front of the building was jammed with vehicles and media personnel. Captain Sheppard, Chief Webster and a number of others were standing behind a cluster of microphones on the sidewalk with their backs toward the building. Jon and Mike walked through the door and joined the group. The two detectives said in unison, "Good morning." The captain looked at his watch and the chief replied, "Morning." Sheppard leaned toward Jon and said in a whisper, "Don't forget our meeting at 10:30."

"Right," Jon whispered back.

Chief Webster leaned over to a young man whom Jon recognized as a media technician and said something. The technician walked up to the microphone, tapped it and turned toward Webster, giving him a nod. Webster, who had asked the technician to make sure the microphone was working, then walked up to the microphone and said, "Thank you for coming. I called this news conference to make an announcement. I will read a prepared statement and will not take any questions at this time." He cleared his throat. "Last night, some time between 8:00 and 10:00, Roger Moreland was found dead in the garage of the Crossroads Mall. Currently the details of how he died are being evaluated by the medical examiner's office. Roger was a dear friend to many in this city. He was a devoted family man, and a wonderful mayor. He will be greatly missed." His voice cracked and his eyes watered. He cleared his throat and said, "I want everyone to know we are going to vigorously investigate this case to bring a speedy closure to this most tragic incident. Thank you." He turned and quickly walked into the building. There was an uproar of questions from the crowd of reporters that went unanswered. The captain, Jon, and Mike followed the chief into the building without responding to the crowd. Mike and Jon went straight to their office where Mike walked over to the corner and poured a cup of coffee asking, "Do you want one Jon?"

"Yeah," Jon replied walking over and holding out his cup. They went back and sat down at opposite sides of the conference table. Jon got up and went to the white board where he picked up a black marker from the tray. "Lets make a list of what we know and what we don't know."

"Okay," Mike said, "We know he was killed before ten and according to the coroner's judgment, as early as eight. Also, he was hit on the head, stabbed six times in the back, held by the neck from the rear, and dragged back out of sight.

"And possibly robbed, Jon added.

Jon had made a nice neat list in the upper left corner of the board with the heading 'KNOWN FACTS'. "Now," he said, "lets make a list of what we don't know." He turned and wrote 'UNKNOWNS' on the other side.

Mike said: "Why was he killed, who killed him, what kind of knife was used, why was he at the mall, was he alone, the exact place he was killed. "And the exact time he was killed, Jon said." Jon had recorded the list on the board and then added, "Did he have enemies and who were they, did he have insurance, how much, and was he fooling around."

"Well, that's a start," Jon said. "It's ten thirty, lets go see the captain." He picked up the surveillance tape from the table and as he slipped it into his pocket, said, "We'll take a look at this tape on the captain's machine this morning."

CHAPTER FOUR

(Wednesday)

When they walked into the captain's office, he was on the telephone with the chief of police, Paul Webster. He motioned for them to take the two straight chairs in front of the desk. The two chairs were the only places besides the captain's chair that weren't piled full of papers. It always amazed Jon how the he ever found anything. Every square inch of his desk, credenza, file cabinets, and conference table was covered with papers. Not just a few papers spread around, but piles of paper varying from six inches to over twelve inches high. It looked like a major clean up campaign staging area where someone was trying to decide what to throw away and what to keep and had sorted every thing into piles that weren't very neatly stacked. But in all the time he had worked for Sheppard, he never knew his boss to lose anything. As they sat down, they heard him say, "Yes sir, I've got my best team on it and I am going to make every resource available to them. Yes, sir. I understand. You can count on it. Good-by." Slamming the phone down, he said, "Damn, that's the part of this job I hate." He ran his fingers through his gray wavy hair, and then wiped his hands over his round face and worked his index fingers into his eyes trying to clear the visible signs of stress from his face. "I've been on the phone for a half hour with the chief listening to how I should and shouldn't do my job. Also, he would like the case solved last week. Well that's my problem. What can you tell me, Jon?" Sheppard asked.

"Not much. We've sorted out the facts and the unknowns, plan to make a list of possible suspects immediately after this meeting, and start interviewing people this afternoon. He summarized the lists of facts and unknowns for him and gave him a run-down on what they had seen at the crime scene the night before. He reached into his pocket and pulled out the tape, saying, "We have a security surveillance tape from the mall we want to look at," Jon said, as he handed him the tape. Sheppard put it in the machine and pushed play, as the detectives pulled their chairs around the end of the desk closer to the TV.

The picture came on showing the mall door from a camera viewpoint above and in front of the door. There was a running clock timer in the lower left hand corner of the screen. At 9:15:20 p.m. two people came out the door and walked towards the camera and disappeared from the screen. At 9:20:05 p.m. the mayor came through the same door and turned left out of the picture. At 9:22:28, the screen went blank.

"Shit," Jon said.

"Well, the security guard told you it didn't show anything." Mike said.

"Play it again, Captain," Jon requested

This time everybody sat forward and stared intensely at the screen.

"What's that? Mike asked.

"What?" Jon said.

"Back it up. There, at 9:20:35.

"Back it up again."

"There, stop it."

At 9:20:35 p.m. there was something on the door glass.

"A reflection." Jon said, "as the door was closing, but, I can't make out anything. It was just a flicker."

They looked at it a dozen times and no one could see anything distinguishable. When they stopped the frame and looked at it, they seemed to see less.

Jon took the tape out of the machine.

"Oh, by the way," Sheppard said, as they started to leave, "I meant what I said to the chief. If there is anything you need let me know immediately."

"Okay," they said in unison as they walked out the door.

On their way back to their office, Jon said, "Right, 'Anything we need', That'll be the day."

Back in the office they returned to their lists. Jon went to the board and wrote 'SUSPECTS'.

"You go first," he said to Mike.

"The wife, the son, and the city council members. Who else?" Mike asked.

Jon said and wrote: "The mall manager, the mall owner, some politician., and a girl friend, if he had one."

"Why the manager and owner of the mall?"

"Because, the pending expansion I've been reading about in the papers could be a factor." There had been recent articles in the papers that the mall was going to be doubled in size and would include a multistory hotel. Also, there were proposed plans to build an aquarium adjoining the mall and plans to develop an inner harbor district on the canal leading to the lake. Advocates, including the mayor and some of the common council members, claimed that the new development would create a unique tourist attraction and help the economy. Of course, like all things, there were some who thought it was not a good idea. The expansion project was supposed to start any day. They had already gotten approval to close a major city street to accomplish the expansion.

"Yeah, I guess you're right".

"Okay," Jon said, "That's about it. Let's both sit down and make a list of what we think we should do and in what order we should do it." Twenty minutes later they compared lists and wrote the consolidated list, which was short, on the board. This time Mike went to the board and wrote in the lower right portion of the board,'THINGS TO DO'

Jon said, and Mike wrote, "Interview suspects, call medical examiner, call crime lab, and have lunch."

They now had enough information on the board to serve as a guide and help keep them on track.

They decided to make the phone calls, have lunch, and then start the interviewing.

KNOWN FACTS

KILLED BETWEEN 8 & 10 p.m.
STABBED 6 TIMES
STABBED IN THE BACK
HELD BY THE NECK FROM THE REAR
DRAGGED BACK OUT OF SIGHT

UNKNOWNS

WHY WAS HE KILLED
WHO KILLED HIM
WHAT KIND OF KNIFE
WHY WAS HE AT THE MALL
WAS HE ALONE
EXACT PLACE HE WAS KILLED
EXACT TIME HE WAS KILLED
DID HE HAVE ENEMIES
WHO WERE HIS ENEMIES
DID HE HAVE INSURANCE
WAS HE FOOLING AROUND
HOW MUCH LIFE INSURANCE

SUSPECTS

THE WIFE
THE SON
THE CITY COUNCIL MEMBERS
THE MALL MANAGER
THE MALL OWNER
SOME POLITICIAN
A GIRL FRIEND, IF HE HAD ONE

THINGS TO DO

INTERVIEW SUSPECTS
CALL MEDICAL EXAMINER
CALL CRIME LAB
HAVE LUNCH

THE WHITE BOARD

Downtown, not too far from police headquarters, Backus Gibbs had just come home from work and sat in his dark second floor apartment. He lived there alone since he'd left his nagging mother and Baltimore five years ago. He was somewhat paranoid about crowds and didn't like to ride buses or go shopping because of the people. He was a loner and tended to frequent bars that were not crowded; and when he went to a movie, he would sit down front to avoid others. Now he sat in his one room apartment thinking about his actions last night. The darkness of the room matched his mood He was thinking back. He had done a number of jobs for Drango. Mostly, the jobs were just strong-arm tactics to scare people into paying Drango what they owed him. The murdering of the mayor was a first. He had tried to kill a guy one other time in a bar. The guy had given him some lip and Gibbs had taken a swing at him. The guy swung back and knocked out Gibbs' front tooth. Gibbs had pulled a switchblade and went for the guy's chest but he deflected the knife and the knife had cut the man's shoulder. The bartender called the cops and Gibbs spent a week in jail. The guy he knifed spent a week in the hospital. Gibbs thought the bastard should've died. Now he was a killer. It had been a lot easier then he thought it'd be. He reached for the phone and dialed a number.

"Hello."
"Drango?"
"Yeah?"
"This is Gibbs."
"Yeah?"
"It's done."
"I know, I get papers and have a TV."
"Well, when do I get my markers back?"
"When you come and get them, asshole."
"Would today be okay," Gibbs asked."
"I guess," Drango said. "I'll be here until 6:00."

"I'll be right over."

Drango's office was small and located in a run-down and almost empty strip mall on the south side of town. His most profitable massage parlor, Ecstasy, was located in the same mall.

Drango muttered to himself, hanging up the phone, "After he picks up his markers, I don't ever want to see him again." As much as Drango hated Gibbs, he was grateful for the job that Gibbs had performed Tuesday night. To him it was worth many times the twenty-five thousand that he had paid Gibbs to stop the mayor's crusade against his massage parlors.

He went to the small safe in the corner of the office and opened it. He put away the twenty-two thousand in cash that he had just finished counting. It was the weeks take from his parlors. While he had the safe open, he took out the markers that were paper clipped together with 'Backus Gibbs' printed on the top slip. He closed the safe and laid the bundle of markers on his desk. He sat down at the desk, pulled a bottle of scotch from a desk drawer and poured himself a drink in a dirty glass that was sitting on the desk. Then he put the bottle away, sat back to enjoy his

drink and put his feet up on the desk. Then there was a knock at the door. "Come in!" he yelled.

"I've come for my markers, Sid," Gibbs said, as he entered the office.

"Here, take them and get out, Drango said, throwing the bundle of IOUs across the desk. "I don't want to see you around here again." Gibbs picked up the markers and stood looking at Drango.

"What are you looking at?"

"I thought you would treat me nicer after what I did for you."

"Bull shit, I'm doing you a favor, erasing your debt, now get out and don't come back."

Gibbs left the office with his head down looking like a whipped dog. He decided to go home and call his mother.

Winona Gibbs lived in a row house in east Baltimore not too far from inner harbor. She was sitting in the living room with a long time friend, Rita Pansky. "I'll tell you the truth, Rita. I haven't heard from Backus in five years. As you know, he moved into his own apartment in 1991 and I would see him once or twice a week. Then, about two years after he moved out, he stopped coming around. When I hadn't heard from him for about a week and a half, I tried to call and found out his phone had been disconnected. I still haven't heard from him. Backus and I never did have a good relationship, but I do love him and miss him terribly. You're the only person I've told about him going away because I feel ashamed to admit it and feel it was my fault he left. He was never a very responsible or loving son, but I would give anything to just see him again. You're lucky Rita, to know where your kids are and have them call or come and see you once in awhile. Besides you've got three sons, and I've only got Backus."

Cheer up Winona, one of these days he'll call or drop in. Men are like that. My son's aren't always attentive. The two who are married are a lot better and that's because of their wives. The one who's single never calls. If I didn't call and nag him, it's hard to tell when I'd see him.

"How about another cup of coffee Rita?"

"Don't mind if I do."

Winona struggled to remove her one hundred eighty pounds from the overstuffed chair in which she was sitting. The long flowing clothes she wore to help hide her weight didn't help her mobility. Finally upright, she combed her fingers through her grayish-blond hair that was cut like a man's, adjusted her glasses and had just started through the dark dining room heading toward the kitchen for coffee, when the phone rang. She continued through the dining room and picked up the phone in the small hall at the foot of the stairs between the two rooms.

"Hello."

"Hi Mom, it's Backus."

"Oh my God! Backus! Where are you?"

"I'm in Syracuse, New York and I'm working at a golf course."

"Oh, Backus, I miss you so much."

"Do you, Mom? Really?"

"I do, Backus. I was just telling Rita, you remember Rita, that I missed you terribly and would like to see you. I'm so sorry now that you and I didn't get along better. I've had a lot of time to think and I feel I was too hard on you. When are you coming home Backus?"

"Well, Mom, I was thinking about coming to visit if it's ok with you."

"Of course it's ok. When are you coming and how long will you stay? You know I still have your room just the way you left it."

"I thought I'd leave in the morning. I could be there in time for supper tomorrow around five o'clock."

"That would be wonderful Backus, I'll make your favorite, roast beef and mashed potatoes. What would you like to have for dessert?"

"How about apple pie?

"Apple pie it is, and we'll have ice cream with it. Oh Backus, I can hardly wait."

"Ok, Mom, I'll see you tomorrow. Bye."

CHAPTER FIVE

(*Wednesday afternoon*)

Jon picked up the phone book and looked up the mayor's home phone number. He dialed the number and it was answered on the first ring. "Moreland residence," said a female voice with a Scottish accent."

"Is Mrs. Moreland there?"

"One moment please."

"Hello, This is Allecsia Moreland."

"Hello, Mrs. Moreland, I'm sorry to bother you so soon after your terrible tragedy, but this is Detective Lieutenant Broder of the Syracuse Police. First I would like to offer my deepest sympathy on your tremendous loss."

"Thank you," she said in a shaky voice."

"I wonder if it would be possible to meet with you this afternoon? I have a few questions that I need to ask, and I'd like you to go to the morgue with me to officially identify your husband."

"Of course," she said, with a sniffle, and in a quivering voice added, "I'm anxious to see Roger.

"Would two o'clock be okay?"

"That will be fine," she said.

"Thank you, Mrs. Moreland and I'll see you at two. If you would like your son to come with you, it would be okay."

"Thank you."

It was already twelve o'clock, so they didn't have a lot of time because the Moreland's home was way over on the southwest side of town. To save time, they stopped at a Burger King on the way.

The mayor lived at 2442 Hursh Rd. in the Chenango Hills development, not too far from the zoo. The street was a long, tree-lined cul-de-sac and the mayor's house was at the very end in the center of the cul-de-sac. It was a two-story brick house with white shutters and white columns framing the massive oak double-door entrance. There were hemlock trees at each corner of the house, sand cherry bushes under each of the windows and holly covering all the areas in between. The center area of the brick paved circular driveway had a large dogwood tree with ivy ground covering underneath.

Jon parked the truck on the driveway at the front door and Mike parked behind him. They went to the door and rang the bell. An elderly woman with gray hair, glasses and wearing a gray maid's uniform, opened the door.

" Good afternoon," she said, with a Scottish brogue that Jon recognized from his earlier phone call, "may I help you?"

"I'm Detective Broder and this is Detective Crane. I called earlier for an appointment with Mrs. Moreland."

"Yes, come in and wait here while I check with Mrs. Moreland."

After she went through the door to the right, they looked around the entrance. There was a spiral oak staircase and railing that went up to the right around a large crystal chandelier. The stairs were covered in the center with dark green carpeting. Along the wall going up the stairs were five large oil portraits. The floor of the foyer was tiled in white and green marble and the walls were covered with a silk finish wall covering in a pale green and white. It was a very impressive entrance.

The maid came back and said, "Please follow me." They followed her into a large family room where Mrs. Moreland was sitting in a wing back chair near a window. There were two other chairs grouped with the one she was sitting in and there were three other similar conversation areas in the room. One of the groupings in front of a fireplace consisted of a three-seat couch and two love seats. The furniture was all covered in color-coordinated fabrics of pale green. The floor was covered with a number of oriental rugs also in coordinated colors.

Allecsia Moreland was an attractive woman in her late fifties with brown hair and glasses. She was wearing a beige pantsuit with a brown silk blouse. She stood as Jon and Mike entered the room and the maid waited at the door. The detectives crossed the room and greeted Mrs. Moreland, each one in turn taking her hand gently.

Jonathan said, "Mrs. Moreland it is very kind of you to see us."

"Thank you, would you like something to drink?"

"No thanks," Jonathan answered for them both.

Mrs. Moreland told the maid that she could leave.

Jonathan spoke first. "Mrs. Moreland, we didn't know your husband, so we'd like to ask you some questions to get some understanding of him in hopes that the knowledge will help guide us in our search for the murderer. If you're not up to it, or as we go along, if the questions distress you, please let us know and we'll hold further questions."

"Thank you, but I think I'm up to it. I'm anxious to do everything I can to help find Roger's murderer."

"Tell us about your husband."

"My husband was a wonderful man. Kind, gentle and a very smart and honest Politician."

"Did he have any enemies?" Mike asked.

"I don't know of any," she said, but I'm sure there were people who were affected one way or another because of my husband's politics. He ran his life based on honesty first and peoples beliefs, feelings and actions second. But if he had real enemies, I don't know who they were. He tried to protect me as much as possible from his political life." Her voice cracked and she started to sob. After she had blown her nose and calmed down, Jon asked, "Did you and your husband get along well Mrs. Moreland?"

Allecsia Moreland looked out the window and took some time before she spoke.

"I met my husband in high school while he was on the football team and I was a cheerleader. We met at a booster's club dance where he asked me to dance. The following week we were going steady and we were married while Roger was in college. That was forty years ago." She started to sob again and wiped her nose, as she said, "Yes we got along very well and were still very much in love."

Jon paused a few minutes and then asked, "Where were you last night between eight and ten p.m.?"

" Here at home alone."

"Did anyone call you or did you call anyone?"

"No."

"I believe you have one son. Is that correct?"

"Yes, his name is Tom."

"Did your husband and your son get along well?"

"Oh, they had some differences but all in all, they got along pretty well."

"What kind of differences?" Mike asked.

"Well, Tom has his own construction business and his father didn't always approve of the way he ran the business. Roger was very conservative and always felt that Tom was extravagant and sometimes sloppy in the way he operated the business."

"Did they ever fight?" Jon asked.

"No they argued a lot but never really fought about it."

"What was the mayor doing at the mall so late last night?" Jon asked.

"He had a meeting. He called me from the office about six and told me he had a meeting and wouldn't be home until about ten. He didn't say with who the meeting was or where it was to be. It was not unusual for him to call and say he had a late meeting. So I didn't think any thing about it. That was the last time I talked to him and I never saw him again." She sobbed, tears dripped down her cheeks and she blew her nose.

"Mrs. Moreland, I know this is painful for you so that's enough questions for now. Perhaps later when you have had a little time, we can talk again. Now, I have to ask you to accompany us down to the morgue to make the official identification. Did you want your son or someone else to accompany you?"

"I'll call my son Thomas and he'll meet us there."

Jon and Mike stood, as did Allecsia Moreland. Jon said, "We'll see ourselves out and wait for you out front."

She said, "I'll be right out."

They turned and left the room.

Outside, Mike said, "I'll drive and we'll leave your truck here."

At the medical examiner's office, Jon introduced Mrs. Moreland and her son to Doc. Towsen and the five of them walked into the morgue together. Just inside the door, The ME said, "Mrs. Moreland, if it would be easier for you, we could do this with a photograph."

"No," she said in a quivering voice, "I want to see my husband."

"Very well, follow me." He led the way to the far left wall, which contained rows of two-foot-wide by two-foot-high drawers of stainless steel. He stopped in front of one of the drawers about half way down the wall. He slid the drawer out exposing the sheet-covered body. Mrs. Moreland started to sob uncontrollably as she held a handkerchief to her nose. Towsen said, "Mrs. Moreland, are you sure you wouldn't rather look at a photograph?"

She shook her head as she continued to sob, and said in a shaky nasal twang, "I'll be all right, I want to see my husband." Towsen pulled the sheet back enough to expose Moreland's face.

"Oh my dearest Roger!" she cried, as she sobbed hard enough to cause her shoulders to jerk up and down. She buried her face in her son's shoulder and after a few minutes, the sobbing subsided a little and she was able to say, "Yes that's my Roger and she buried her face in her son's shoulder again and cried without restraint for several moments. After she became calm, Jon said, "Come Mrs. Moreland. We should leave now. After she was back in her son's car, Jon said, "It's three-thirty, Mike, why don't we pick up my truck and drop into the mayor's office and see who's there."

City Hall was a four-story sandstone structure with a red roof and turrets on each corner giving it a castle look. The building took up the small block bounded by Montgomery and Market Streets on the west and east and by Water and E. Washington Streets on the north and south. Jon and Mike found a parking space on Montgomery Street and entered through the E. Washington Street entrance.

They walked up the granite steps to the arch covered landing and entered through the weathered double oak doors with leaded glass, which put them on the second floor where the mayor's office was located. His office was in room 203, which was straight back at the end of the hall opposite the E.Washington Street entrance.

As they approached the office, they could see a black wreath hanging beside the door.

When they approached the office a secretary in a cubicle to the right of the door asked, "May I help you."

"Yes, we're from the Police and would like to speak with whoever is in charge now."

"That would be Mr. McCully. He is, er...r, was the mayor's assistant. Just a minute and I'll see if he can see you" She picked up a phone, pushed a button, and said, "I have two gentlemen out here from the police who would like to see you." When she hung up the phone, she said, "You may go in," as she pointed to the door to her right.

As they entered the office and walked across the room, the man with brown hair behind the desk stood up. He appeared to be in his early forties, was slightly over-weight, and wore a gray pinstriped suit, white shirt and a red paisley tie. He came around the desk and extended his hand, saying, "I'm Jerry McCully."

After introductions, Jon said, "We've been assigned to investigate the mayor's murder and would like to talk to you, if you have some time."

"Of course, please have a seat," he said, pointing to a couch against the wall. Mike and Jon sat down and McCully took a seat in one of two small wing back chairs across a coffee table from the couch.

"Mr. McCully," Jon asked, "do you have any idea who would want to kill your boss?"

"No," he said, "I don't. He was such a nice person. He hardly ever had a bad word to say about anyone."

"How about political enemies?" Mike asked.

"Well there were some people who didn't always agree with the mayor, but I can't think of anyone I'd call an enemy or could have murdered him."

Who didn't always agree with him?" Mike asked.

"Well, there was Councilman Frank Richards, Councilman George Walthers, City Court Judge John Thomas and City Auditor Barry Johnson" "They weren't enemies, they just didn't see eye to eye on budgets and some issues."

"What kinds of issues?" Mike asked.

""The biggest issue was the expansion of the Crossroads Mall. The mayor was in favor of the expansion and the councilmen and Johnson were against it. The councilmen thought the area already had too much shopping and Johnson thought that it would cause budget problems. The mayor however was looking at the bigger picture and felt that the expansion, when completed, would be a tremendous tourist attraction and would be a big asset to the city and surrounding communities."

Jon said, "Was the mall expansion the only thing the mayor had disagreements with people about?"

"Of course not, but it was the biggest issue because of the magnitude of the project."

"What else?"

"Well, Johnson argued with the mayor constantly about the budget. Anything that took money."

"What about the judge?"

"The mayor refused to support the judge during the last election because the mayor thought the judge was too liberal."

"I see," Jon said.

"Do you know if the mayor had an insurance policy?"

"Yes, it's a fringe benefit of the office."

"How much and who is the beneficiary," Jon asked.

"I'm not sure," McCully said, "but I assume his wife is the beneficiary. You'll have to ask Barry Johnson about that, he should know, or at least know who the insurance company is."

"Mr. McCully, did you like your boss and get along well with him?"

"Yes, he was a great guy to work for."

"Where were you last night between eight and ten.?"

"I was home alone."

"Did you call anyone or did anyone call you?"

"No."

"What happens to the mayor's job, since Moreland is dead?"

"I get the position until the next election which is three years away."

"Will you get a pay raise?" Mike asked.

"Yes."

"How much?" Mike asked.

"About twenty-five thousand dollars."

"Jon stood up and Mike and McCully followed his lead. "Mister McCully," Jon said, as he held out his hand, "thank you for your time, you have been very helpful."

As McCully shook his hand, he said, "Any time."

"We will very likely be wanting to talk to you again," Mike said, as he extended his hand. McCully shook his hand and said, "I want to do everything I can to help find Roger's killer. Please call me as often as you like." He walked over and opened the door.

On their way out Jonathan stopped at the secretary's desk. "Are you or were you Mayor Moreland's secretary?"

The attractive blond haired secretary said, "Yes my name is Nancy Brown."

"Nancy, when and where does the Common Council meet?

"They normally meet every other Monday at one o'clock and they meet upstairs in the Council Chamber, room 304. Sometimes they reschedule the meetings to the evening. They are scheduled to meet tomorrow night at seven thirty."

"Thank you, Ms. Brown and have a nice evening."

Outside, Jon said, "Mike, I think we should plan to attend that council meeting tomorrow night and see if they talk about anything related to the case. That means that tomorrow will be another long day. Therefore, since it's six o'clock, and we're beat from lack of sleep last night, let's go upstairs and check out the council chamber and then call it a day."

"No arguments from me," he said as they headed for the stairs.

The council chamber was a fifty-foot square room

with raised oak paneling half way up the walls and over the entire ceiling. The walls were painted ivory and contained a collection of Patsy J. Falvo photographs commemorating the one hundred fiftieth anniversary of the city. As they faced the front of the room, there was a wall of windows on their right. The left wall and the rear wall each contained double raised panel oak doors that opened into the room from the hall. Curved across the front of the room on an eight-inch high platform were ten small oak raised panel desks. Each desk had a microphone and each was labeled with the name of the council member who sat there. The center desk was also labeled 'President' in addition to the name, Jack Wilson. In front of the row of desks was a horseshoe shaped table with oak chairs and microphones. The room had gray carpeting with a burgundy fleck, oak pews with burgundy pads, an aisle down each side and an aisle down the middle. There was a small podium to the right side of the room up front with a microphone attached. The room was empty when Jon and Mike looked in so they entered through the back door and looked around.

"Pretty nice room."

"Yeah, now we know where some of the tax money goes.

"Have you been to City Hall before Jon?"

"First time. You believe that, and I've been a cop here for twenty-five years. How about you."

"Same. Seen enough?"

"Yeah, lets go."

Gibbs went to a Mobil filling station to get some pizza and fill the car with gas so that he could leave very early the next morning for his trip to Baltimore to visit his mother. "Boy, I'm glad I called her," he thought, as he was pumping the gas. She sounded like she really misses me and wants to see me; maybe I shouldn't have waited so long to call. I wonder if she'll treat me better when I visit since she didn't yell at me once on the phone? He paid for the gas, bought three slices of pepperoni pizza with extra cheese, and headed home to pack some clothes.

CHAPTER SIX

(*Thursday morning*)

The alarm went off at six o'clock scaring Gibbs out of a deep sleep. He thrashed around in the bed trying to find the noise and knocked the clock on the floor in the process. "Shit!" He yelled, as he rolled out of bed feeling in the dark trying to get his hands on the ringing clock. He stopped the alarm and sat down on the edge of the bed to calm himself, reaching for the remote control and turning on the TV.

" . . . the rain will turn to snow around noon and it will continue snowing through the evening hours. The storm is moving slowly to the east and should be out of our area by midnight. Snow accumulations of one to three inches are expected in some areas. Now back to Sharon." Turning off the TV, he said aloud, "Shit, that's all I need," and to himself thought, I guess I better get started, and maybe I can miss the snow. He dressed, picked up the bag he had packed last night and ran down the stairs to the car. Outside, it was dark, cold, and raining like the devil. He headed for the interstate hoping he would be able to drive out of the rain and evade the worst of the snow on his way to Baltimore.

Jon and Mike sat in the office looking at the board.

"Well, we had lunch, so we can erase that."

"Yeah," Mike said, laughing. "And after the interview with Mrs. Moreland, I think we can take her off the suspect list."

"At least for now, Jon shrugged, as he erased the two items. Besides, if we change our minds, we can always put her back on." When he had finished updating the board, he said, "Mike you call the lab and I'll call the medical examiner."

"Hi Doc, this is Jon Broder. Have you got the autopsy report on Moreland for us?"

"I have," Towsen said, "And the knife wounds didn't kill him. He was dead before he was stabbed."

"What does that mean?" Jon asked.

"Either the killer didn't know he was dead, or he was a wacko. At any rate, the six knife wounds didn't do anything except make him bleed a little. The blow on the head killed him. That's why the quantity of blood was less than I would expect for that number of wounds. Some of the blood drained into the body cavities because the body was laying with the wounds up. Mostly, though, with the heart stopped when the wounds were inflicted, the quantity of blood was much less than it would have been if the heart were still pumping."

"Anything else I should know?" Broder asked.

"The knife had serrations on the back edge, indicating a fishing knife. The blade was narrow and about seven inches long. That's about it. He had a little alcohol in his blood but basically everything else was in order and unremarkable."

"Thanks Doc, send us a copy of the report right away."

"It's on the way, good-by."

"Crime Lab, The voice said."

"Who is this?" Mike asked.

This is Tom Wilder. How may I help you?"

"Tom, this is Mike Crane. I'm one of the detectives working on the Moreland murder."

"I know who you are," Wilder said.

" Do you have anything for us?"

" I've completed my report."

"Well? . ." Mike asked.

"Well what?"

"Did you find anything that might be helpful to us?"

"Read the report."

"C'mon, Tom, I'll read the report when you send me a copy, now give me a heads-up."

"The report is on its way and the only thing we found that might mean something is a bloody shoe print and a cigarette butt. Nothing else."

"Anything unusual about the?" Mike asked.

"The cigarette, no, but the shoe print looks very unusual. It was a crescent-shaped pattern like there was a chunk out of the sole of the shoe. The cigarette butt was a plain old Camel. It might be good for a DNA check later.

"Thanks, " Mike said, hanging up and saying, "Boy, Wilder sure is cocky." After relating the cigarette butt and foot print information to Jon, he asked, " What did the coroner say?"

Jon told him and then said, "Oh by the way, the captain told me he wants to meet with us every morning at ten thirty and it's time.

"Morning Captain," they said in unison as they entered the office and sat down. They briefed Sheppard on the verbal reports from the lab and the medical examiner and told him about the McCully interview and their plan to attend the council meeting.

"Good," the captain said. "Is there anything else?"

"Not right now," Jon answered. "We just need to get to work. We're going to continue interviewing this afternoon. So if it's ok with you, we'll get at it."

"Go," the captain said. "And I'll see you in the morning."

On the way back to the office they decided Mike would interview the son and Jon the judge.

Mike called Information to get the number for Thomas Moreland Construction. The secretary said Moreland was on the job at Fayette and Almond. The first three stories of the six-story building were being renovated. Mike decided to go to the job site unannounced. He said to the secretary, "Thanks, I'll call back later."

Jon called the County Courthouse after looking up the number in the blue pages and spoke to the court clerk

"I'd like to speak with Judge Thomas please."

"May I ask who's calling?"

"Detective Broder, SPD Homicide.

"One moment please."

"Hello, this is Judge Thomas."

"Judge, this is Detective Broder with SPD Homicide and I would like to meet with you and talk about the mayor's murder."

There was a moment of silence and the judge said, "I don't know how I can help, but I'll be glad to see you. When would you like to meet?"

"Right now would be good for me," Jon said. More silence.

"I have a short meeting scheduled but could see you in a half hour here in my office."

"That will be fine. I'll see you in a half hour."

Mike pulled up to the job site on the corner of Fayette and double-parked, put his 'OFFICER ON DUTY' tag on the dash, and went into the building. He walked over bricks, broken concrete blocks, old boards and other debris to get to the first workman he saw and asked him where he could find Moreland.

"I think he's on the third floor."

"How do I get up there?"

"The stairs over there."

"No elevator?"

"Yeah, there's an elevator, but it's not working"

"Shit," Mike muttered as he headed for the stairs. The place was dangerous. It had been stripped back to the bare brick and there were piles of rubble and broken wood everywhere, including the stairs, and the air was thick with dust. Not a very healthy place to work, he thought as he started up the stairs.

On the third floor, he approached two men leaning over a set of blueprints spread out on a piece of plywood set on top of a high set of sawhorses. One man was dressed in a sport coat and the other one had on dirty Jeans and a blue denim shirt. Both men wore yellow hardhats.

"Thomas Moreland?"

"I'm Moreland," the tall heavyset man in the sport coat said. "

Mike put out his hand, introduced himself and said, "I'd like to talk to you about your father's death."

Moreland shook his hand. "What do you want to know?"

"Why don't we go someplace where it's a little quieter and cleaner. Like the coffee shop a couple of doors down the street"

"Look,"Moreland said, "I don't have a lot of time. I should be home with my mother to help her cope with this thing, but I had to come to work long enough to keep the job going. I've got a penalty clause in the contract, and if the job isn't finished by the deadline in the contract, it costs me a thousand dollars a day."

"It won't take long," Mike said.

As they were leaving, Moreland turned and yelled over his shoulder, "I'll be back in a few minutes, Moe. Get started on those changes."

"Yes sir."

They went into Manny's Coffee Shop three doors down from the job. The shop was long and narrow with a row of stools at a counter on one side and a row of tables for two against the wall on the other side. The floor was black and white tile and the walls were bare brick. They sat down at one of the tables and a waitress with bleached hair, wearing an apron, came over and put place mats on the table. "What can I get you fellows?"

"Coffee."

"Make it two."

After the waitress left, Mike said, "Mr. Moreland, I want you to know that I am very sorry about the death of your father."

"Thanks."

"What can you tell me about your father?"

"My father was a good mayor and was well liked."

"Was he a good father?"

"What do you mean?"

"Well, your Mother said you and your father argued sometimes. Did you like him? Did you and he get along?"

"What are you insinuating, Detective?"

"I'm not insinuating anything. I just want to know how you and your father got along."

"We got along fine. But sometimes he forgot that I'm a grown man and have the right to make my own decisions, whether he liked them or not. Mostly, our disagreements were about how I ran the business. Even though it wasn't any of my father's concern, he periodically liked to put in his two cents worth. Basically, he was very conservative and I wasn't afraid to take some risk to get ahead. Regardless, I loved my father and he loved me. End of speech."

"I'm sure that's true, Mr. Moreland. Understand that I have to cover all the bases for the record. That's the nature of my job. Now, where were you between eight and ten on the night your father was killed?"

"I was in my office that night from seven until eleven. I was with my foreman Moe Dagerty. We didn't even go out to eat; we had sandwiches sent in and worked straight through. You can ask him."

"I probably will," Mike said. Did you call anybody while you were working?"

"Yes, I called my wife about eight o'clock and told her that I would not be home for dinner and would be working late. You can call and check with her if you like."

"I probably will, thanks."

Jon parked his car on Montgomery and walked over to the courthouse. He checked his gun and went through security. He took the elevator to the second floor and entered room 224 where he found a very attractive black secretary wearing a red dress sitting at a desk just inside the door. "Hi, I'm Detective Broder, and Judge Thomas is expecting me."

"One moment." She smiled at Jon as she went towards a door behind her desk to his right.

Returning after looking in the open door and nodding, she said, "You may enter."

The judge was sitting behind a large oak paneled desk, which had glass covering the top. As Jonathan approached him he rose, came around the desk and extended his hand, saying, "I'm glad I could accommodate you, Detective, my schedule is not always as flexible as it is today."

John Thomas was a short soft man whose hair had turned an unbelievable white. He sat down at his desk and said, "We're all very distressed about this horrendous crime. What can I do to help?"

"I understand that the mayor didn't support you in the last election, and wondered if there were hard feelings between you."

"Nooo. . .," he said, "Roger and I didn't always agree because he was an ultra conservative in almost all things. The pending Mall expansion was one of the few progressive ideas that the mayor embraced."

"So there were no ill feelings between you?"

"No, there were just many issues where we didn't agree."

"Give me a couple of examples."

"I thought criminals should be punished according to the crime regardless of their age. Roger thought young offenders should have special treatment. He thought the arts, theater, museums, etc. should have very low priority in the budget and I thought they should be very high.
Things like that, hardly life threatening issues."

"I would agree," Jon said.

"Judge, can you think of anyone who might have had a motive to kill the mayor?"

" I've been racking my brain ever since it happened and honestly, I can't. In spite of our differences, Roger Moreland was a good and sincere person who was liked by everyone. There were only two groups of people in town that are exceptions. First, Roger, at times intimidated anyone who did not take care of their property. Also he had just recently started on a campaign to clean up pornography and prostitution in the city. Specifically he had targeted the massage parlors, and had already closed a couple."

"Do you know anything about his relationships with his staff or the Common Council?"

"No, I don't."

Jonathan stood up and said, "Thank you Judge, for your time and help. I really appreciate it, and I may contact you again."

"Oh by the way Judge, where were you between eight and ten Tuesday night?"

"I was home with my wife watching TV."

"Thanks."

"Any time", the Judge said as he stood. "I want to see the murderer brought to justice, and I will make myself available anytime to help achieve that end."

There had been a lot of snow and freezing rain in the Pennsylvania hills around Scranton. The roads had been extremely slippery, and slowed the heavy traffic to a crawl in many places. Gibbs had taken the northeast extension of the Pennsylvania Turnpike north of Wilkes Barre in order to by-pass road work through Scranton. Shortly after getting onto the bypass, he was driving by a stretch where the bank on the right consisted of a rocky slope with a row of skinny white birch trees along the top that looked like a crooked picket fence. Just as he was coming to the end of the sloping rock area a deer jumped out and ran across the road in front of him. He hit his breaks and started to slide but missed the deer by inches. The car slid sideways for a while then fishtailed first right and then left and caught the berm before he slowed enough to get the car under control and come to a stop. Gibbs sat for a few minutes shaking before he was able to continue on. The going had been slow all morning, but now, the rain and snow had finally stopped. Although the roads were now generally clear, there were still some slippery spots, causing the traffic to continue to be slower and heavier than normal. It was still cold, overcast, and felt like it was going to snow again at any minute. Gibbs was approaching Harrisburg and, seeing a sign for McDonalds, decided to stop for lunch. He needed a break.

CHAPTER SEVEN

(*Thursday Afternoon*)

"How did you make out with the son?" Jon asked Mike as he walked across the office and poured a cup of coffee.

"I feel that he wasn't involved. It seems to me that his relationship with his father was normal. Like all fathers, the mayor kept forgetting that his son wasn't a little boy any longer and was quite capable of making his own decisions and running his business. Oh, Tom Moreland got upset with his father from time to time, but I think he really loved his father. How did you make out with the judge?"

"Same. He had some differences with the mayor, but I don't see any motive for murder. He did tell me something that I think we should look into further. The mayor was apparently on a real campaign to clean up prostitution and pornography in the city."

"Yeah, I did read something in the papers awhile back that he had already closed a couple of massage parlors."

"The judge confirmed that."

"Now what," Mike asked.

Jon got up from his desk, walked over and updated the board.   Sitting back down at his desk, he said, "I haven't been able to stop thinking about that damn video tape. We know there's something on it if we could somehow see it. Last night, I thought of something we might try. Channel 2 television station has a video lab that is supposed to be the best in the country. I think we should talk to the captain and see if he will agree to let me contact them to see if they'll help. What do you think?"

He'll probably have a fit. Shit, he doesn't even like to go to other law enforcement agencies for fear of losing control.

"Yeah, I know, but maybe I can sell the idea on the basis of their expert capability and closeness. We don't have anything to lose by asking. Lets go see him. Then when we finish, with him we'll go see the two city council members who McCully thinks didn't get along with Moreland.

"Good afternoon Captain," they chimed, walking in and sitting in front of his desk.

"How are we doing?" Sheppard asked.

"Slow, we've talked to Judge Thomas and to Moreland's son today, nothing jumps out.

"Captain, could you talk to the chief and see if he knew of any real political enemies that Moreland had?"

"Sure," Sheppard, said. "I talk to him every day. I'll let you know tomorrow. Now, what else?"

"You remember the tape?"

"Of course, what about it?"

"I'd like your okay to make contact with a person at the channel 2 television station and see if I can get access to their video lab."

"Jon, are you crazy?" Sheppard yelled.

"I know how you feel, Captain, but that tape hasn't given us anything. And you know that the TV 2 lab is the best in the country. Even the FBI people told us that last year."

"Yeah, I know Jon, but if the thing got out of control, I could be in big trouble."

"I know, but trust me, I can control it. I'll have to give them something, but I'll make it small and keep it under control, I promise."

"You're right about the tape, It's worth nothing to us or anyone the way it is. If they're able to pull something from it, you've got to make sure it doesn't get out."

"I can handle that," Jon said.

"Who's your contact?" Sheppard asked.

"I thought I'd call Jessica Mathews. She's very professional, I trust her and she's got a great rapport with her station manager."

"Well, ok, Jon, but you better believe that you could very well be playing with my job."

"I understand Captain, and you don't have to worry."

"Yeah, right. Go on get out of here before I change my mind and I'll see you tomorrow."

They went back to their own office and set up the interviews with the Council members. They agreed on the way back to the office that Mike would talk to Walthers and Jon would take Richards. They were both able to set up interviews for one o'clock.

Jon picked up the phone and dialed. "Operator, I would like the number for the TV 2 news room. As he wrote the number on the desk pad, he asked, "Can you dial it for me?" He waited. "Hello, I'd like to speak with Jessica Mathews, please."

"One moment please."

"She's not here right now, she's out on an assignment."

"Can you get a message to her and have her call me right away?"

"Yeah, give me your name and number."

This is Jonathan Broder with the Police Department. My number is 445-6224. This is very important, have her call me right away."

"Right."

He hung up.

After a few minutes of discussion, they decided to go to the Barbecue for lunch. It was close by on Clinton St. and was famous for both it's food and memorabilia. The phone rang and Jon answered it, recognizing Jessica Mathews' voice. "Hi, Jess," Thanks for calling. I need your help."

"Shoot" she said.

"How about lunch or dinner?

"Boy, this must be heavy."

"It's important and I'd like to talk to you in person about it."

"Okay she said, lunch."

"Where?"

"How about Bravoes on Taft Road?"

"Okay, I'll meet you there at twelve."

Hanging up the phone, he said, "Mike you'll have to go to the Barbecue by yourself, but I'm still going to do the one o'clock interview after lunch, and I'll meet you back her later this afternoon. Also, don't forget we have the council meeting tonight."

"Yeah, I'll see you later."

Jon arrived at Bravoes before Jessica and waited, enjoying the warmth being given off by the fireplace at the entrance. He heard the door open at twelve-fifteen and turned to see her standing there looking beautiful. She had on dark gray slacks, a light gray silk blouse with mother of pearl buttons. Her silver and turquoise jewelry accentuated the buttons on the blouse. Jon hadn't seen her in a couple of months and her shoulder length blond hair was longer than the last time he saw her. The curls fiaming her face enhanced the beauty of her pug nose, soft lips and narrow chin.

" Hi Jon. It's good to see you again."

"The same here. How have you been?"

"I've been great, how about you."

"Good.

After being seated, a waitress approached them and smiling, said, "Hi, Jess, you haven't been here in a long time."

CLYDE SKAGGS

"Hi Carol, I guess it has been a long time considering I think you make the best hamburger in town."

"What can I get you to drink, Jess?

She ordered water, Jonathan coffee and then Jessica asked, "What's so important, are you going to give me something on the Moreland case?"

"As I mentioned on the phone, I need your help, and it does involve the Moreland case. We don't really have a good lead yet, but yesterday, we found something on a security surveillance tape. The trouble is, it's just a flicker, and we can't make it out. I know that TV 2's video lab is the best in the country. So what I need is for you to set me up with your lab boys to work on the tape."

"Hold it!" she said emphatically, holding her hand up palm out. "You know how the station manager feels about others using our lab."

The waitress came back with their drinks and waited to take their order.

"I'll have a burger, medium-well, with lettuce, tomato, and mayonnaise and an order of fries. Also a coke."

"And you, sir?"

"The same thing less the coke and more coffee."

"Thanks, I'll put your orders in right away."

"I know Jess, but you need to make an exception here."

"Why?"

"Because we need the help, but more importantly to you and your station, I'll give you an exclusive lead over everyone else if the information we get from the tape leads to something." "What do you think's on the tape?" she asked.

70

"I have no idea, that's why I need help."

The waitress was back with the coke and coffee.

"What do you say?"

" I'll have to talk to the station manager and get back to you. I think for an exclusive lead, he'll go for it."

"Can you talk to him today?"

"As soon as I get back from lunch."

The food came, and they ate in silence. Afterwards, Jon asked for the check, paid it and they left. As they parted, Jessica said, "Thanks for lunch."

"Your welcome, and Jess, I've got a one o'clock interview, but should be back in the office about three. Call me as soon as you have word. I'd like to come in today to work on the tape, if possible."

" I'll do what I can."

Jon climbed into his truck and headed for Richards' office.

Mike parked and walked to the Barbecue. It was a mad house as usual, but he was able to get a table. The short round waitress with curly brown hair brought a menu and asked what he wanted to drink. He ordered a coke. When she came back with the drink he ordered a pulled pork sandwich with extra barbecue sauce and French fries. While waiting for his food, Mike looked around the restaurant and wondered where they had found all the junk in the place. Old metal signs, old license plates, a broken lawn mower, a partial set of golf clubs with wooden shafts, an old lantern, an old bottle capper and it went on and on. The waitress brought the food and took his mind off the junk. The sandwich was almost four inches high. He took

71

the top half of the bun off, applied a generous amount of barbecue sauce and dove in. It was messy but really good. When he finished his lunch, he dropped a dollar on the table for a tip, and went to the bar to pay the bill. He went to his car and proceeded to the parking lot of One Lincoln Center. He went inside the building by a side door facing the parking lot and checked the directory for the law offices of Jorgason, Simpson and Prince, which was the law firm where George Walthers worked. When he reached the Sixth floor and stepped off the elevator he found a receptionist's cubicle to his immediate right. As he walked up, a petite woman with white hair and round rimless glasses said, " May I help you?"

"My name is Micheal Crane and I have an appointment with Mr. Walthers.

"Just a moment and I'll check."

She picked up the phone, pressed a button and told Walthers he was there. "You may go right in. It's the first door on your right around that corner."

The office seemed almost as big as Mike's house. There were windows floor to ceiling on two walls and the other two walls were paneled in a light cherry wood and contained bookcases. The desk sitting in the middle of the floor towards one corner was large and complemented by a round cherry conference table in front of the windows and a large leather couch and two chairs in front of the bookcases. As Mike entered the office, Walthers stood up. He was in his early sixties with white hair trending to baldness. He had on a blue suit with a white shirt and red tie with white polka dots. He moved to the end of the desk, smiled, and extended his hand. "Detective Crane," he said, as they shook hands, "what can I do for you? Please have a seat."

Mike sat down in front of the desk and crossed his legs as Walthers returned to his desk chair.

"I'm trying to find out as much information about the mayor as I can, and thought you might be able to help. How did you and the mayor get along?"

"Fine."

"McCully told us that you disagreed with the mayor about the mall expansion."

"I did. But that was just a case of us doing our jobs. The mayor thought the mall expansion would be good for tourism and I thought we already had too many malls. Yes, we disagreed but that had nothing to do with his death."

"What kind of man was he?"

"He was an honest mayor and always had the best interest of the city in mind. I just think that he was wrong sometimes. The mall was one of those times."

"Can you think of anyone who would want him dead?"

"No I can't, but he was trying to clean up the city and the Council has been working on legislation to make it tougher for massage parlors to get away with prostitution. I don't know what kind of opposition he was involved with on that front. Not too friendly would be my guess."

"Do you have an alibi for Tuesday night between eight and ten p.m. Mr. Walthers?"

"Yes, my wife and I went out to dinner. We left home about seven thirty and got back about eleven o'clock. We ate at the Texas Steak House."

"Ok, how did the mayor and his family get along?"

"I can't answer that. I didn't socialize with the mayor or his family. I've been to a few parties where he and his wife were in attendance and they seemed to be a very loving couple."

"You've been very helpful Mr. Walthers, please call me if you think of anything that might help. Here's my card."

CHAPTER EIGHT

(Thursday afternoon)

Jonathan found a parking place on Genesee St. about a block from the bank where Richards worked. The parking space between a van and a pickup truck was very tight and it took him several tries and much maneuvering to squeeze into it. He walked back along the low hedge that separated the lawn in front of the bank from the sidewalk and entered the bank through the front door. Inside, he saw two desks in the open area, a row of teller cages opposite the entrance and doors to offices on the other two sides. He went to the desk nearest to the offices on the left.

"He introduced himself to the petite blond with a ponytail and said, "I have an appointment with Frank Richards."

"One moment, please." She smiled, getting up from her desk and heading down the row of offices. Her ponytail swished from side to side almost in sync with her hips as she walked to one of the office doors and stuck her head in. Returning to her desk, she said, "He'll see you. It's the third door down."

Richards was sitting behind a small mahogany desk that looked even smaller than it was because of his size. When he stood, it was obvious that he was over six feet and carried his two hundred pounds very well. After introductions, Jon said, "I'm investigating the Moreland murder and I'm trying to get background information that might help shed some light on the case. What can you tell me?"

"Roger and I happened to run into each other at City Hall that morning and decided to meet for lunch at Chester's. We exchanged views on the mall expansion, each of us trying to sway the other on our positions. I was opposed to the expansion and the mayor was in favor of it. Neither of us would change our position and we parted company around one o'clock. He did tell me that he was going to meet Tuesday night with the mall manager, Arthur Hill, to discuss some of the details of the expansion plan. He didn't tell me what time, but I have a feeling that he was leaving that meeting when he was attacked."

"Do you know of anyone who would want to kill him?"

"No. He and I didn't agree on everything but he was the kind of person whom everyone liked and he was doing a good job as mayor. His clean-up campaign against the massage parlors in town was certainly a controversial issue. The council has been working on legislation for some time that will severely restrict the activities of the parlors and the proposed legislation, was passed last week with a vote of seven to two."

"Tell me about the controversies and who voted against it."

"The two women on the council, Priscilla Fischer and Dorothy Jamison, voted against it. They felt that the city should not be permitting and licensing a business that it really wanted to get rid of. They pointed out that we have a law prohibiting prostitution and a one hundred year old education law that requires anyone working on the human body to have a license. They feel that those laws should be enforced. And, of course, the licensed therapists, fifteen of whom came to one of our Council meetings, wanted the legislation scuttled for the license reason, in order to protect their turf. Most of the members of the common council agree that the ordinance is flawed, but an ordinance in Rochester like the one we just passed reduced the number of parlors there from twelve to two. That's a number that makes it easier to catch anyone providing sexual services for a fee. The new ordinance, which takes place next month, requires parlor operators to buy a two hundred dollar permit that subjects them to background checks and surprise police inspections. Police can cite an operator when an employee is caught giving a body rub without being clothed. We've only had one owner, Sidney Drango, appear before the council but he owns a bunch of parlors, including the Ecstasy on the south side of town. He said the notion that parlors are havens for prostitution makes him mad. He claims that his employees must state in writing they provide nothing other than body rubs in their private time with clients, when both are typically naked.

Yeah, right! The guy who runs his place, Carl, was at the meeting when the ordinance was passed. He called the council members jerks, and stomped out of the meeting. Drango says that he'll pay the two hundred dollars license fee and ask for approval allowing the women to wear bikinis while they work. I wish him lots of luck!"

"Do you think this parlor issue is serious enough to kill over?" Jon asked

"I don't know, but I wouldn't think so. Most of these places work outside the law and take their chances on paying a fine if they're caught. With ten or more parlors in the city, it's very hard to police them all and we don't catch many."

"Where were you Tuesday night between eight and ten p.m.?"

"Home, alone."

Did you talk to anyone during that time?"

"No."

"Okay," Jon said, handing him his card, "Thanks for your help and call me if you think of anything else."

Back at the office, Jon said to Mike, "Let's see if we can go see the mall manager this afternoon." Mike looked up the number, read it to Jon and he dialed.

"Hello, this is Arthur Hill."

"Mr. Hill this is Jon Broder with the Syracuse police and I would like to make an appointment for my partner and me to meet with you and talk about Roger Moreland's murder. I realize it's short notice, but we have some free time right now if you could see us."

"Of course, I'll make time. When would you like to come over?"

"It's a little after two now, how about three o'clock?"

"That would be fine, I'll see you at three."

Immediately after Jon hung up, the phone rang and it was Jessica Mathews.

"Hi Jess, how did you make out?"

"It's your lucky day Jon, the station manager agreed to let you in the lab and the technician, Frank Salvo, says he has some time now if you can be here by two thirty."

"No problem, will you be there?"

"Yes."

"Ok, I'll meet you there in fifteen minutes and, hanging up, he asked Mike, "Can you handle the Hill interview by yourself?"

"Sure, what's happening?"

"Jess got me into the lab at two thirty, so I have to leave right now."

The TV 2 facility was located just north of the city in a small strip mall. The video lab was in the same building. When Broder arrived, Jessica was waiting for him in the lobby.

"Hi Jon," she said.

"Hi Jess, I really appreciate what you've done for me."

"I'll give you plenty of time to show how much," she retorted. "You owe me big time."

"Let's hope we find something," he said, following her through a door off the lobby and down a long dark carpeted corridor containing two doors on the right side and three doors on the left. They went through another door at the end of the hall into a room filled with equipment. Sitting in front of a TV monitor, was a man in his early thirties with brown curly hair down over his ears, wearing jeans, dirty sneakers, and an orange Syracuse University sweatshirt. He turned toward them as they entered and stood up.

"Hey Jess."

"Hey Frank, I want you to meet Detective Jon Broder."

"How do you do, Detective," Salvo said as he extended his hand.

"I'm good, Frank, and I really appreciate you seeing me."

"Glad to help if I can. Jess tells me you have a tape that needs working on."

"Yeah, all I can see is a flicker and I'm hoping you can turn it into something." He reached into the side pocket of his blue sport coat, pulled out the tape and handed it to Salvo.

"Let's see what we can do," he said sitting down and inserting the tape into a VCR slot over his head. "First I'll copy the tape into the computer and give you back the original." He worked the mouse and pushed several buttons causing the image to come up on the screen at eye level, and the tape was ejected. He handed it back to Jon, saying, "We won't need this any more now that it's in the computer."

Putting the tape back in his pocket, Jon yelled, "There!" as the flash of the image came and went.

Frank Salvo let the tape finish, returned to the beginning and played it again in slow motion. When he got to the frame with the reflection, he stopped it and said, "First, I'll enhance it."

The image became bolder.

"Yeah," Jon said, "that's better."

"Can you make it bigger?"

Salvo put a frame around the image on the glass and punched another button. The image on the glass filled the screen, but was still ghost-like.

"It's hard to tell anything about it because we're looking through it," Jon remarked. "Can you do anything about that?"

"I can adjust the contrast," Salvo said as he pushed a button.

"That's better, Frank, let me look at it for a minute." Jon sat down along side Frank and studied the image. "It's definitely a face," he muttered.

"Yeah, look," Frank said, as he pointed at a spot on the screen. There's his mouth, you can see his teeth, and there's a dark spot right there."

"Yeah, I see, what is it?"

"I don't know," Frank replied. Let's see what we can do." Using the mouse, he put a frame around the mouth and it filled the screen. Then he pressed several buttons in succession and the dark spot was very visible as a missing tooth.

"I'll be," Jon said. "The guy's got a tooth missing. Can you give me a printout of that?"

Frank pushed a button and the printer to his left groaned as it spit out a sheet of paper.

"Frank, I'd like for you to go back to the view of his head. I think he's wearing a hat. Maybe we can see something there."

Frank nodded his head as he manipulated the equipment. The man's head filled the screen.

"Give me a printout of that too. Maybe the police artist can use it to create a sketch of the guy." Frank pushed a button and the print was out before Jonathan finished his sentence. "Now, blow up the portion around his hat".

Doing as Jon had asked, Frank said, "Let me reduce the brightness and increase the contrast."

When he finished, the image was clear enough to make out.

"What is it?" Jon asked.

"It looks like a semicircle with a spike sticking out of it."

"Enlarge the spike area," Jon requested.

"I'm a son of a bitch!" he said after Frank enlarged the area. "I think it's a pine tree coming up through that semicircular area.

"I've seen that before, someplace . . . where? Is that lettering under the emblem?" he asked.

"Yeah, it looks like it, but it's too faint to read. Man, we're pushing the limit, but let me optimize the contrast and brightness once more and see if it helps." He pushed several buttons and shook his head. "I guess we've done all we can. Whatever the lettering is, it's too near the tone of background to bring it out. I'm sorry, man."

"Hey Frank, he said shaking his hand, "you've just given me the first real lead in this case and I can't thank you enough. Now, if you can give me a copy of the enhanced image on tape, I'll get out of your hair and let you get back to work." He stood up, gathered the printouts, and taking the tape from Frank that he had copied while they were talking, said, C'mon, Jess, let's go."

Outside, he asked Jess, "How about having dinner with me tomorrow night so we can talk about pay back? I'd ask you tonight, but I have to go to a council meeting at seven thirty."

"Ok," she said," What time and where?"

"How about Simone's on Erie Blvd. at eight o'clock?"

"Good, you want to pick me up, or do you want me to meet you there?"

"I'll pick you up at seven thirty, here, he said, handing her an open notebook and pen, write down your address and phone number." She did as he instructed and handed the book and pen back.

"If I should get hung up tomorrow and run late, I'll call you.."

She smiled and waved to him as she got into her car.

CHAPTER NINE

(Thursday Afternoon)

The offices at the Crossroads Mall were located on the third floor opposite the theaters. The manager's office, the person at the information desk said, was on the third level to the right as you get off the elevator.

Mike went up the glassed in elevator looking down at the lower level area as the car went up. He was thinking about two other deaths that had occurred inside the mall. They were both declared suicides by the medical examiner. The most recent one was a seventeen-year-old boy, who was high on amphetamine tablets. Many were shocked to find out that it was a somewhat common practice for teens to use large doses of over-the-counter drugs to achieve highs. The other death was a despondent middle-aged woman who just decided to end it all. They had both jumped forty feet from the movie level to the tiled concrete floor of the lower level.

The elevator opened and he exited into a tiled hallway. He looked both ways, saw the theaters to his left and headed down a carpeted hall to his right that led to a desk. He told the lady at the desk that he wanted to see Arthur Hill and she directed him to the end of the carpeted hall where Hill's office was the last door on the right.

When he entered the office marked Mall Manager, he found a small waiting area to the right with a secretary.

"I'm Detective Crane to see Mr. Hill."

"Yes, he's expecting you, please go right in." She smiled, and gestured towards an open door on her right.

Hill was wearing a gray suit, white shirt that appeared too big around his skinny neck and a wildly colored tie that looked like it came from Rush Limbaugh. He was sitting on a couch reading some papers, looked up as Mike approached, and reached out to shake hands without standing. He then suggested that Mike sit in one of the chairs facing the couch and said, "I expected two of you."

"My partner, who called you, wasn't able to make it because something came up as we were walking out of the office that required his immediate attention, so I came ahead without him. We're trying to find out everything we can about the mayor's activities leading up to the time of his death and we had one person tell us that the mayor had a meeting with you Tuesday night. We believe that you are the last person to talk to him before his death."

"Yes, Roger and I did meet Tuesday night about eight o'clock. He wanted to review some of the details of the mall expansion. We had a drink and talked for about an hour and a half before he left a little after nine."

"Did he leave alone?"

"Yes he did."

"Did he seem upset or concerned about anything?"

"No, he was his normal congenial self."

"Did you and the mayor get along well," Mike asked.

"Yes, we agreed on most issues and I was an avid supporter of his."

"For the record, Mr. Hill, what time did you leave the mall Tuesday?"

"I left right behind Roger, within five minutes, and went out by the first floor entrance to the outside parking lot. I found out about Roger's death on the news yesterday morning."

"Do you know anyone who disliked the mayor enough to kill him?"

"No, I don't."

"Thank you Mr. Hill, you've been very helpful."

Mike handed him a business card and said, "If you think of anything that might be of help, please give me a call."

On the way down in the elevator, Mike decided to go talk to security about their cameras."

The guard was sitting in a chair viewing a bank of video screens and when Mike walked in, he turned and stood.

Mike showed him his badge. "I'm Detective Crane with SPD and am one of the detectives investigating the death of Roger Moreland. Can you tell me about the video surveillance cameras in the underground parking area?"

"We have cameras down there, but the one on the door where the murder occurred covers only the door. The murder took place at the corner out of the camera's field of view. We've looked at the tape several times and can't see anything."

" I know, one of the guards gave us a copy of the tape Tuesday night."

"Oh yeah, that was Joe, and he told me but I forgot."

"Can you tell me anything about that night?" Mike asked.

"Well, as you saw on the tape, Mayor Moreland came out the door at nine twenty, and apparently was stabbed shortly after he was outside the camera's view. I have a feeling that whoever did it knew what area the camera covered."

"How would someone find that out?" Mike asked.

"They would either have to know a lot about camera technology or have seen the monitor here. It's possible to see these screens from outside, but of course, they'd have to know which screen to look at."

"Thanks a lot, you've been very helpful."

"Anytime," the guard said. "Good luck."

Mike was already in the office when Jon got back from the TV 2 video lab.

"Hey Mike, how'd you make out with the interview?"

"Nothing." Mike said, "He's clean and didn't

contribute anything. How did you do?"

"Our first break, I think. The image we saw on the tape was a man. Probably the killer. We've got two things to go on. First, the guy has a tooth missing in the front and second, he had a ball cap on with an emblem on it. Are we lucky or what? What are the odds of that guy being in the right place for that door to catch his reflection, and even more, what are the odds that he would be looking in the right direction for the glass to catch him straight on?"

"Don't knock it," Mike said, leaning back in his chair, sipping a cup of coffee. "What was the emblem?"

"I'm not sure. It looks like a pine tree through a semicircle. I feel that it looks familiar."

He spread the printouts from Salvo on the conference table. Mike slid his chair over so he could get a good look at them.

"This one," Jon said, pointing to the enlarged head, "I want a sketch artist to look at and see if he can create a sketch of the guy." Then Jon pointed to the printout of the tree, and remarked, this is the picture of the emblem on the hat that looks familiar. It's four o'clock and we've got the council meeting at seven thirty. I think we should get a sketch artist in to work on these printouts and skip the meeting if necessary. What do you think?"

"Yeah, the sketch is more important."

"Okay, lets go see the captain and show him the tape."

Sheppard was slouched back in his chair with his fingers intertwined and his hands resting on his considerable belly. "What's up?" he asked."

Jon handed him the tape and said," Here's the tape that you saw before, only now it's been enhanced. As they watched, the captain said, "I'll be." The reflection was now clearly a person wearing a ball cap and it was also clear that one of his front teeth was missing.

"I want to take this over and show it to the chief. I'm sure he'll want to hold a news conference. What do you think?"

Jon spoke up. "I think a news conference is okay and we should say that we have a clue that could lead to the identity of the murderer and say that in the interest of the investigation, we can't give any further detail at this time." Mike added, "If we say anything more the guy might go deep into hiding and we'll lose him. If we leave it very vague, he may think we're blowing smoke and remain complacent.

"Now," Jon said, "I think we should give something to TV 2 for the eleven o'clock news tonight and hold the news conference at eight o'clock tomorrow. We owe it to TV 2, because without them we wouldn't have the lead."

"Yeah, Sheppard said, "I think your right and I think I can sell it to the chief. Now, what else?"

"You promised us help if we needed it. I think we should have someone from vice to help us look at people related to the massage parlor clean up campaign that the mayor was working on. We have a couple of names from the interviews we've had with members of the Common Council. Also, I think we should have two more detectives to help us do surveillance and stake outs related to the massage parlor angle. What do you think Mike?"

"We may need more later, but I agree that three

should be adequate right now."

"That seems reasonable," Sheppard said, as he picked up the phone. "I'll call Joe Murphy, Special Investigations Division right now." He dialed a number and waited.

About a month ago Murphy had called Sheppard for help and said, "Al, we've had Tony Scossi under surveillance for a long time trying to nail him on either prostitution or drug charges and aren't really making any progress. The problem is, he's very smart and we just can't get close enough. I think the only way we're going to get him is to plant someone in his organization. Since he knows all the vice cops, I'd like to borrow someone from you, a new face, so to speak. Can you help me out?"

"How about Jimmy Scotari? He's worked undercover, handles himself well, and has had a little vice experience, plus he just finished a case and is available." Murphy was grateful, asked Sheppard to send Scotari to see him, and that one day he would return the favor.

Murphy was sitting at his desk drinking a cup of coffee and studying a report that he had just received from one of his detectives. It was a report on the Scossi case and was not good news. He had been successful in getting Scotari into Scossi's organization, by giving Scotari a phony police record and cover story that Scotari had heard about Scossi's activities while he was in prison. In the three weeks that he had been under cover though, he had not been able to come up with a single piece of incriminating information. The only thing new that he reported was that Scossi seemed to have some kind of close relationship with a guy named Sidney Drango. Scotari reported that Scossi and Drango had met a number of times, but he had not been able to find out what the meetings were about. Murphy's thick brown eyebrows seemed to be screwed into his wrinkled brow, his jaw was set, and his lips were tight. That Drango seemed to be involved in everything and they could never get anything concrete against him. The phone rang, causing him to start and he relaxed a little as he answered it.

"Hello."

"Hi, Joe, this is Al Sheppard."

"Hi, Al, what's up?"

"I'm calling about the Moreland murder and I need your help. My guys have a couple of leads that fall in the area of Vice, and I would like for you to loan me a good Vice detective for a week or so to give them a hand."

"Ethan Williams finished an assignment last night. Would he do?"

"Yeah," he answered looking at Jon and Mike and nodding his head. "I know Ethan Williams, and I think he would be perfect for the job. The lead detective on the case is Jonathan Broder, and his partner is Micheal Crane."

"I'll have Williams go to Broder's office tomorrow at nine o'clock."

"Thank you, I'll tell them." Sheppard hung up and said, "Ethan Williams will be in your office at nine tomorrow morning.

"That's great," they both chimed in unison. "What about the other two detectives?" Jon asked.

I think Jay Stern and George Pool have just come off an undercover assignment and are available."

"Good. All right with you Mike?"

"Yeah, I've worked with both of them before and they'll be great."

Sheppard said, "I'll call their lieutenant and tell him to have them in your office tomorrow morning at nine o'clock. Is there anything else?"

"There is one thing, Captain. We want a sketch artist to look at the tape today and make us a sketch of this guy. So, could you give the tape back to us this afternoon in case we need it?"

"That shouldn't be a problem. I'll show it to the chief right away and you can pick it up when we're finished."

Jon and Mike stood up and turned to leave the office. "Oh, by the way Jon, Sheppard called as they reached the door, I want you to field the questions at the news conference tomorrow."

"Thanks a lot," Jon muttered, as they headed for their office.

"Mike, you make a pot of coffee while I call the Crime Analysis Section to see if we can get a sketch artist this afternoon. Also I want to call Jessica."

He called Jessica first. "Hi Jess, I have good news for you. I talked to the captain and got the okay for you to announce the lead on the eleven o'clock news. All you can say is that you have learned from a reliable source that the police have a lead in the Moreland case that could eventually lead to the identity of the murderer. That's all. I know it's not much, but as more information becomes available that we can release without jeopardizing the investigation, I'll see that you get it first. There will be a press conference tomorrow morning at eight o'clock to make an official statement, and we will say the same thing I just told you. Ok, bye."

He called Joe Schmidt in the Crime analysis Section. "Hi, Joe, this is Jon Broder in Investigations. Fine, how are you? Good. Joe, we need a sketch artist for a little while. This afternoon, if possible. You have? Great! You just made my day. Yes, Sully would be perfect. We've worked with him before. Oh, we have some prints from videotape that we would like turned into a sketch. Well, the prints and the tape are not the clearest material we've had, but we hope it's enough to work with. Yeah, five o'clock would be good. Thanks, Joe. Good-by."

As he hung up, Mike walked in after getting the tape back from Sheppard. "We're lucky Mike. Sully Morrison just finished an assignment and will be here at five."

"That's five minutes," Mike said.

Jon and Mike had just gotten coffee and returned to their desks, when they heard a knock at the open door. Jon turned around from the video printouts that he had been studying, and seeing Sully standing at the door, called out, "Hey Sully, come on in." Jon stood up as Mike walked over and they both shook hands with the artist.

CHAPTER TEN

(Thursday Afternoon)

Sully Morrison was in his late fifties, had a white goatee, and white unruly hair that hid his ears. He was a Syracuse native and had graduated from Syracuse University with a degree in Fine Arts. He'd struggled for many years trying to make his mark as a portrait and then a character sketch artist with limited success. Finally, at the age of thirty-two, when he decided to get married, he took a part time job with the police department as a sketch artist to augment his income.

"What can I do for you fellows?" he asked.

Jon took the printouts from his desk and laid them on the conference table, pulling another chair up to the table and suggested that Sully sit down. "These. Printouts," - he spread the pictures out on the table - "came from an enhanced video surveillance tape that we got from the mall security people. The tape's also available if you need it. We think that one's a picture of Moreland's murderer. We hope you can give us a better idea of what he looks like."

"Well . . ." Sully drawled, as he stroked his goatee and studied the pictures, I've had better material to work from." He reached down beside his chair and pulled a twelve by fourteen inch sketchpad and pencil from a bag that he had set on the floor as he sat down. He laid the pad on the table and started to sketch. He used light strokes, but the images from the soft pencil appeared bold. "First," he said, as he sketched, "we'll get the shape of his head down. That's pretty clear from the photo. Also, I can see some detail on his right ear, the lips, the nose, and the jaw." he said, continuing to sketch. Mike and Jon looked on in fascination at the quickness with which he worked, Jon asking, "Do you still work part time for the department, Sully?"

"Yeah, my art is selling well enough now that twenty hours a week is all I want." Sully added the detail of the left front broken tooth and moved up to add the baseball cap. "Well, there it is," he said standing and stepping back to evaluate his work in comparison to the photos he had   worked from. He reached down and added the emblem to the front of the cap. "You know," he said; as he stroked his beard again, "I think that's the logo that Sunset Pines uses."

"Damn," Jon and Mike exclaimed in unison, as Jon slapped the table top and declared, I knew that emblem looked familiar."

"It should, Mike said, we've played golf there enough times. I must have at least three of their hats at home in the closet with that logo on them."

"Yeah, me too" Jon added.

"Well, Sully said, standing, that's about all I can do for you."

"You can't imagine how much you helped by identifying that stupid logo, Jon said."

"Glad to be of service." Sully smiled, tearing the sketch off the pad and proceeding to put the pad and pencil back in his bag. They shook hands and as Sully was going through the door, Jon called, "I'm going to have our captain call your boss and tell him what a great job you did."

"Thanks," Sully answered, as he nonchalantly raised his left hand in the air and disappeared around the corner.

"Hey, Jon, it's only five forty and it stays light until about seven thirty. Why don't we go out to the golf course and see if they recognize the sketch?"

"Yeah, I was thinking the same thing and we could grab a sandwich at the clubhouse when we finish."

"No," Mike said, "I think I'd better go home right after we finish. I've really been neglecting the family since this case started. As a matter of fact, I'd better call Martha now, he reasoned out loud, and turned around to his desk picking up the phone.

"Hi Hon, it's me, he said in a hushed tone. I wanted to let you know we're working late again tonight and I should be home about nine. Why don't you put Jimmy to bed early and we'll have a late candlelight dinner. I'll stop and bring home some Chinese."

"Sounds good. I'll see you at nine."

It was exactly six o'clock when Jon and Mike met outside the clubhouse at Sunset Pine golf course. The sun was setting and the sky in the east was brilliant orange streaked with gray behind the trees. As they entered the Pro Shop and approached the tall thin man at the counter wearing jeans and a green sweater, Jon pulled out the Xerox copy of Sully's sketch, he'd made before leaving the office, and showed it to him.

"Do you recognize this guy?"

"Who's asking?"

"The police," Jon said as he flashed his shield.

The man looked at the sketch and said. "Yeah, I think I do. That might be a guy who cuts the grass here. I don't know his name though, You'd have to ask either the owners or the Pro about that."

"When will they be here?" Jon asked.

"They're usually here by seven thirty every morning. What's this about?"

"We've got some questions for the guy. Do you have the names of the owners and the Pro?"

"Yeah, the owners are Joyce and Fred Preston and the Pro's Chris Jorgason."

As Jon wrote the names in his notebook, Mike asked, "How about phone numbers for them?"

"Yeah, I can give you that." He turned around to the counter behind him and wrote the numbers on a business card that he picked up from the counter. "I wrote the owner's number on the back and the Pro's number is printed on the front," he said handing the card to Jon who already had his cell phone in his hand.

After introductions, Jon said, "Mr. Preston we have a sketch of a person whom we think works for you and we want to ask him some questions in connection with a murder. We'd like you to look at the sketch and see if you can identify him. We can either come to you or you can come to us here at the golf course, whichever would be best for you. That's great. We'll wait right here in the clubhouse." After Jon hung up, he announced to no one in particular, "Preston lives close by and is coming right over." Mike looked at his watch and to the counter man, asked, "Is there coffee at the bar?"

"Yeah."

"Come on Jon, it's only six-fifteen, I'll buy you a cup of coffee."

They had just gotten their coffee and seated themselves at a table when a man in his late sixties wearing jeans, sweat shirt and sneakers, strode towards them from the Pro Shop.

"Are you the detectives?"

"Yeah," Jon answered, as they stood up.

"I'm Fred Preston."

"Jon shook his hand saying, "Here's the sketch I mentioned on the phone."

Preston took the sketch and immediately nodded his head up. "I'd say that's Backus Gibbs. He cuts grass for us. The shape of the jaw and the missing tooth are easy to spot. I told Jorgason we shouldn't hire him."

"Do you have an address for Gibbs?"

"Yeah, out in the Pro Shop. I'll get it."

"If you have any other information such as next of kin or telephone number, bring that also."

He looked back over his shoulder and said, "I have the phone numbers and addresses, Chris Jorgason, the Pro, has all the personnel records."

He was back in a few minutes with the phone number and address.

"Thanks Mr. Preston, for the information, and for coming over."

"My pleasure. Do you think Backus Gibbs is the killer?"

Instead of answering, Jon said, "We have some questions for him and we appreciate your help. Thanks"

On the way back to their cars, Jon gave Mike a high five and said exuberantly, "Can you believe our luck? I wonder though, why would a grass cutter want to kill the mayor? Course we don't know for sure that he's the one, but it seems to me that for his reflection to be on that glass, it has to be him. Also, how many suspects could there be with that tooth missing? I'm inclined to proceed on the basis that he's the guy, and figure maybe there's also someone else involved."

Mike said, "That makes sense to me," and asked with a grin, "Are we going to go see Mr. Gibbs?"

"Right now, why don't you follow me?"

They pulled up in front of a two-story brick building at the address on Salina given to them by the golf course owner and both found parking spaces on the opposite side of the street. When they entered the building they found a small hall at the foot of a flight of stairs and two mailboxes on the wall. The mailbox marked 2A had Backus Gibbs' name on it. They went up the stairs and knocked on the door. There was no answer, so they banged louder. From behind them, they heard, "Are you looking for Gibbs?"

"Yeah, have you seen him?"

"No, but the bastard ran down the stairs this morning at seven o'clock and woke me up."

"If you didn't see him how do you know it was Gibbs?"

"Because he never has visitors and there wasn't anybody here when I looked out. I haven't seen anybody visit him in the five years he's lived there, he's a loner."

"Thanks mister."

He pulled his head in and closed the door.

"Should we talk to him, Jon?"

"No, let's wait. I don't want him to know we're cops in case Gibbs comes back. You watch the apartment while I go get something to eat and call the captain. I'll be back to relieve you by eight and take the first watch while you go home, eat, and get a few hours sleep. Then, you can relieve me about three. You won't have to attend the news conference or the meeting with the detectives in the morning unless Gibbs shows up and you arrest him. If he does show up, call me before you call for backup, so I can be in on the arrest. I'll take care of the news conference at eight in the morning, meet with the detectives at nine, and, if you don't show up, I'll send Stern and Pool over to relieve you. I'll be back shortly."

Jon went to a deli, ordered a roast beef, and while it was being prepared, sat down at a table and called the

captain.   He asked for a large black coffee to go and left
the deli at seven-twenty in the rain to relieve Mike.

CHAPTER ELEVEN

(*Thursday afternoon*)

The weather had cleared during late afternoon and it was a quarter to four when Gibbs exited the interstate onto the Baltimore Beltway heading west. He had decided to take the Jones Falls Expressway south to Orleans Street and take Patterson Park Avenue to Baltimore Street. He would be there in about a half hour and was nervous about seeing his mother again after being gone for five years. He could hardly believe how nice she had sounded on the phone. Maybe she had changed and really did miss him. He thought about their relationship during the drive down and decided that the problem wasn't all his mother's fault, he could have done better and tried harder to please her while he was living at home. Maybe things would be better now. He would soon find out.

*   *   *

Winona Gibbs lived in the second house from the end of a group of row homes in the block across Baltimore Street from the north side of Patterson Park. The Gibbs house had tan imitation stone on the front and the steps were painted brown. There was a brown awning over the front door and the window along side. Backus parked on the side street and walked to the corner. Before turning to the left towards his mother's house, he stood and looked across the street at the park. He remembered how much fun he and his friends had as kids playing in the park. He shook his head to get his mind back on the task at hand and walked on towards his mother's house and up the steps. He knocked on the door, which had plastic moldings painted gold so they would stand out and make the door look like it was paneled. Trying the knob as he knocked, he found it locked. He waited only a couple minutes when the door was opened and he stepped in to face his mother.

"Hi Mom, I thought maybe you weren't home when the door was locked."

"Oh Backus!" she cried, throwing her arms around his neck and squeezing him to her large soft body. "Oh, Backus, Backus, I'm so glad you came home, give me a kiss." He backed away, looked into her tear filled eyes, and gave her a gentle kiss on her tear-streaked cheek. She hugged him again and wept as she held him tight for several moments.

After calming a bit, she took his hand, pulled him into the living room, and closed the door. He sat down in a chair and she sat on the couch to his right. There was a plastic topped coffee table in front of the couch and a recliner and table on the wall opposite the couch. The TV was on the front wall between the door and window. The drapes were closed and with the awnings over the door and window the room was dark, even though a lamp was lit on the table between the chair Backus was sitting in and the couch.

"The door was locked because the neighborhood's not as safe as it used to be," she said. "How have you been, Backus?"

I've been okay; I've got a good job cutting grass at a golf course. I get a lot of fresh air and can play for free when I'm not working."

"I didn't know you played golf, Winona remarked. "When did you learn?"

"After I started working at the course. Mostly, cause it was free and I found out they had clubs I could use for nothing. It gives me some exercise and doesn't cost me anything."

"What happened to your tooth Backus?"

"I slipped on the ice, and fell," he lied. It couldn't be fixed, and cost too much to replace, so I had it pulled.

You should have it replaced. If you don't have the money, maybe I could help. Do you have a girl?"

"No, no girls, I think I'm better off without them."

"Are you hungry, Backus? I've got a roast beef in the oven and I can have dinner on the table right away if you're hungry."

"Yeah Mom, I am hungry, starved, as a matter of fact."

"Okay, I'll get it ready." She hoisted herself from the couch, took Backus' head between her hands and gave him a big kiss on the lips. Would you like a cup of coffee while I'm getting dinner ready?"

"Yeah, that would be nice."

After Backus had three helpings of roast beef and mashed potatoes, he pushed himself away from the table, saying, "Man, that was the best meal I've had since I left home. Thanks, Mom."

"You're welcome." His mother beamed, and asked, "How about a piece of apple pie with ice cream for dessert?"

"Oh Mom, I'd love to, but can we wait a little while? I'm really stuffed."

"Sure, why don't you go turn on the TV while I clear the table, then I'll join you."

"It can't get much better than this," Backus thought, just before he dozed off while watching the news.

Mike was about halfway home, after being relieved by Jon, when he stopped and ran quickly through the rain into the Chinese take-out. He ordered cashew chicken, sweet and sour pork, and steamed rice. While the food was being prepared, he went next door to a liquor store and bought a bottle of Chenin Blanc wine. When he got home Martha came to meet him, put her arm around his waist, and they walked to the kitchen together. He set the food and wine on the counter and took her in his arms and kissed her thinking how much he had missed her all day. Pulling back, looking into her eyes and smiling, he said "Boy did I miss you today."

"Me too." She grinned, feeling pleased that he

missed her.

"I'll fix us a drink and we can sit down for a few minutes. Is wine okay?" he asked.

"Fine," she said reaching in the cabinet for glasses while Mike found the corkscrew. Opening and pouring the wine, he handed one glass to Martha and took the other one with the bottle and led the way to the living room. He set the bottle and his glass on the coffee table along side the candle that Martha had burning, and sat down on the couch. Martha plopped down beside him, placed her glass on the table, wrapped her arms around his neck and gave him a lingering kiss.

"Now, how was your day?" she asked.

"We had a great day." He explained about the artist sketch and the golf course logo that led them to where the guy on the tape worked. " We talked to the owner of the golf course who identified him as one of their grass cutters. We got his name and address and went to arrest him. The bad news is that he wasn't there and even worse, I have to relieve Jon on the stakeout at three a.m."

"Oh . . ." she moaned.

"Now, what do you think, should we have sex before we eat or after?" he asked.

"Let's finish our wine and then decide," She picked up her glass, clinked his and they drank. They talked a little about Martha's day and about Jimmy and after they finished the wine, Mike asked, "can you heat the Chinese in the microwave?"

"Sure."

"Okay," he said, taking her hand, rising, and tugging gently. As she stood, he started towards the bedroom and she followed close behind. When they reached the bedroom they left the light off, stood for a while kissing, then hurriedly undressed each other before they fell onto the bed with an urgency that neither one had experienced for some time. Afterwards, they rolled over in a state of exhaustion. They rested awhile, then embraced, kissed, and started to get aroused again. "What do you think? Should we take an interlude for some Chinese?"

"We've got a microwave," Martha said, breathing hard and climbing on top of him. "It can wait."

It hadn't been long since they 'd made love, but tonight seemed special. Martha thought it was mostly the anticipation caused by Mike's phone call earlier, but it didn't hurt that they'd both had a good day and the wine probably helped. Finishing dinner at ten thirty, they went to bed and slept well until the alarm went of at two thirty.

"Any action Jon?" Mike asked as he opened the car door and got in.

"Nothing, I haven't seen a soul since you left. I think he's skipped and after the meeting tomorrow, I'll call the golf course and see if he has any next of kin or references listed in his personnel file. I'm bushed, Ill see you tomorrow, Mike."

"Good night."

Maggie was sound asleep in the recliner when Jon entered the living room. He went over to her knelt down and stroked her side. She rolled over on her back, yawned, and stretched. He scratched her belly and said, "C'mon Maggie, let's see what we can find for you to eat." She ran

107

ahead of him to the kitchen and sat looking up in anticipation. Jon opened the cabinet and pulled out a small can of red tuna. "A special treat tonight, Maggie, because I'm so late." He put the tuna in her bowl and set it on the floor. She downed it in gulps while she alternately groaned and purred. "You enjoy," he said, "I'm going to bed."

CHAPTER TWELVE

(Friday morning)

It was a beautiful sunny morning. The cold front that had moved in Thursday had passed through and was on it's way towards the coast. The weather on the morning news said that the temperature today was going to reach the forties.

The chief of police, Paul Webster, had gotten up early, showered, shaved, brushed his teeth, and polished his black shoes. He dressed in his best blue suit, a pale blue French cuffed shirt and put on a blue and red striped tie. His wife had been awake off and on while he was getting ready and was asleep when he was ready to leave the room. He kissed her on the forehead without waking her and headed for the kitchen to get a cup of coffee.

His wife no longer bothered to get up in the mornings to see her husband off. He always left very early and she found that it made her days seem too long and lonely. Therefore she would prepare the coffee pot the night before and set it on automatic so the coffee would be ready at seven a.m.

The chief got a cup of coffee from the pot and took it to the family room where he stood looking out the window thinking about the scheduled news conference and how much he enjoyed being in front of the cameras and how it would help his aspirations to become governor He had advised the news media in advance of the eight o'clock news conference to be held on the steps of City Hall to discuss the Moreland murder. He wished he had more information to give them. He finished his coffee, looked at his watch, and headed for the garage to drive downtown. He would stop at a restaurant on the way and have some breakfast.

When Jon arrived at City Hall, the street in front of the entrance was crowded with news media personnel, equipment and vehicles. He saw the chief and the captain standing at the top of the steps near the front door. The sidewalk at the base of the steps was surrounded by a solid mass of news reporters. He pushed his way through the crowd, and seeing Jessica on the way, smiled at her but didn't stop to talk. Everyone was yelling out questions that were ignored as he pushed on through and up the steps. "Good morning Captain, Chief Webster," he said. They returned his greeting.

Webster stepped up to the microphone that had been set up on the arch covered landing at the top of the stairs and flashes were going off all through the crowd. "He raised his hands with his palms facing the crowd to indicate that he wanted them to be quiet. "Ladies and gentlemen, thank you for coming. This news conference will be brief. I will read a short statement and then we will take a few questions." He pulled a folded piece of paper from his pocket, opened it, and started to read. "With the help of the Crossroads Mall security personnel we have uncovered our first lead in the Moreland murder case. Of course we can't give you any specifics on the lead because that would impede our investigation, but I will say, that although this lead has not yet resulted in any arrests, it is our belief that it will only be a matter of time until we catch the murderer. I'm sorry I can't tell you more, but thought I should let you know we feel progress is being made. Now, I would like to turn the microphone over to Lieutenant Broder, who is in charge of the investigation and will answer your questions." He stepped back and Jonathan walked up.

As Jon approached the microphone everyone was yelling at the same time and flash bulbs were still popping through the crowd. He pointed to a young man near the front of the crowd.

"Do you know who the murderer is?"

"No."

"Do you . . . When will . . . what kind . . ." Jon pointed to a female on the right side of the crowd.

"When will you make an arrest?"

"It's too early to tell at this time, but we feel the information we have will eventually lead to an arrest. "You," Jon yelled, as he pointed to his left.

"How did TV 2 get this information for the eleven o'clock news last night before all the rest of us?"

"I don't know."

111

Next he pointed to Jessica Mathews, "Jess?"

She smiled and said, "When will you have more information for us?"

"As you know we hold news conferences as often as we can to keep you informed. We will continue to do that as releasable information becomes available. The yells erupted again and Jon held up his hands. "That's all we can tell you at this time and we thank you for coming." He turned and joined Sheppard and Webster to go into city hall. Jon waited five minutes and then left City Hall by the Market Street door to avoid the reporters. He had to get back to the office to meet with the other detectives.

He arrived in the office before anyone else and updated the board while he was waiting.

Ethan Williams was the first of the detectives to arrive.

"Come on in Ethan," Jonathan said rising to greet him. Ethan's big ever-present smile softened the effect that his two hundred twenty pound frame, lumberjack beard and gruff voice gave when you first met him. Just as they sat down, the other two detectives appeared at the door.

"Is this the crime convention we were asked to attend," the skinny one asked, smiling and leading the way into the office. "I'm Jay Stern," he said as he held out his hand to Ethan whom he hadn't met before. As they shook hands, he nodded towards the tall guy with blond curly hair who was right behind him. "This is my partner George Pool."

"Hi George."

Jon then pulled a fourth chair up to the table, saying, "Glad to have you guys on board." Before getting comfortable, they all got coffee and then came back and sat down. "As you probably all know, " Jon said, "you're here to give us a hand on the Moreland murder case. What you don't know is that last night we determined the name of the person who we think committed the murder.

"We also have another guy named Sidney Drango, a massage parlor owner, on our 'SUSPECTS' list and he's the reason we brought Ethan in from vice.

Now, here's where we stand. The name of the suspect we identified last night is Backus Gibbs and my partner, Mike, is watching his apartment as we speak. We went to arrest him last night and he wasn't home. We think he might have skipped, but thought we should keep watch on the apartment just in case. So, Jay, and George, I would like for the two of you to relieve Mike so he can go home and get some sleep, and then, the three of you work out a schedule to keep the apartment under twenty four hour surveillance until we catch the guy. Ethan, I'd like for you to follow up on Drango and the massage parlor angle. According to the people we've interviewed, the mayor had worked with the common council to pass legislation that really put a crimp in the massage parlor business, and Drango didn't like it."

"I know this Drango character," Ethan said. "He's a bad one. He's got his finger in all kinds of illegal stuff. He runs a loan sharking business, is tight with the mob, and has strip joints, massage parlors, and adult bookstores. It's rumored that he launders money for the mob, though, we've not been able to prove it. I'll go talk to him."

113

"Maybe we should bring Drango in here for questioning just to shake him up. If you all look over at the board, you'll see under 'THINGS TO DO' what we feel should be done right away. I'll follow up on Gibbs and work on a search warrant for his apartment. Now if there are no questions, let's get started. Jon stood and reached over to his desk and picked up some papers. He spread the copies of the artist sketch out on the table so that everyone could see them. He explained how the surveillance tape had resulted in the sketch and the hat logo had led to the golf course where Gibbs worked. "Everybody take a copy of this sketch just in case you need it. Let's all meet back here tomorrow morning or earlier, if something develops. Here's my cell phone number," he said, handing each one a card. "Jay, here's the address of Gibbs' apartment and Mike drives a white Honda." Everyone left and Jon headed for Moreland's funeral, which was being held at the Methodist church on Fayette Street.

The cars were already lined up for the funeral. They were stretched out for almost two blocks. He went up the stairs and entered the church sanctuary to find standing room only. He looked towards the front of the church and saw the open casket sitting in front of the altar. The casket was a rich mahogany with polished brass handles and a lining of lavender silk. Mrs. Moreland and her son, Thomas, were standing along side the casket. People were lined up and filing past them. Every few minutes someone would pause, say something, and reach out to take the Morelands' hands in a gesture of sympathy. The son and his mother were both dressed in black. Jon pushed through the crowd and as he started down the aisle, saw Gerold McCully coming towards him. He was dressed in a brown double-breasted suit, a beige shirt and tan tie that had brown triangles in it.

"Good morning Detective. I'm glad to see you here. I think it'll give Allecsia a lift, because she very downhearted today. I saw on the news this morning that you have a lead in the case."

"Yeah, that's true, but we still have a lot of work to do and are a long way from finding the murderer."

"Well good luck, be sure and call me if I can be of any help." He walked toward the back of the church and Jon walked on down the aisle, joining the line until he reached the casket.

"Mrs. Moreland, Mr. Moreland."

"Thank you for coming, Detective," they said in unison, tears rolling down Mrs. Moreland's cheeks.

"Mrs. Moreland, I can much better appreciate your loss after the interviewing we've done. Everyone has spoken very highly of your husband. Even his political adversaries haven't said anything bad about him. I wanted to pay my respects but I won't stay for the service because I still have a lot of work to do to catch the murderer. I hope you understand."

"I do understand", she said, "and we appreciate your efforts, don't we Tom?" She turned and looked at her son.

"We certainly do," he acknowledged, nodding his head. They all shook hands and Broder turned to leave.

Outside, he backtracked along Fayette St. to the parking lot on Montgomery where he had left his truck.

CHAPTER THIRTEEN

(Friday Afternoon)

Jon was back in the office talking on the telephone with Assistant District Attorney Laura Frasier. He had informed her of the identification of Backus Gibbs, the attempted arrest, and Ethan's follow up on Drango.

"Laurie, I need to get copies of Gibbs' phone records for the last month. Can you get the subpoena for me from the Attorney General's office?

"Sure, I can handle the whole thing by phone and fax. When do you think Ethan will bring Drango in for questioning?"

"It should be this afternoon."

"I'd like to be there when you question him, so why don't I work on the phone record problem and see if I can get them this afternoon. You call me when you know what Ethan is doing concerning Drango."

"Okay Laurie, I'll call you later. Bye."

Jon sat down at his desk and prepared the affidavits for a search warrant of Gibbs' apartment. He was very careful to get the apartment address and number accurate, and describe very carefully what he would be looking for. He hadn't gotten a search warrant from Judge Thomas before but knew that most judges were sticklers on the specificity of the information for a warrant. Therefore, based on the information he had received from the medical examiner and the crime lab, he described the knife, blunt instrument, and shoe with a crescent shaped chunk out of the sole, the best he could. He then called Chris Jorgason at the golf course.

Introducing himself, he said, "Mr. Jorgason, I spoke to Mr. Preston last night about Backus Gibbs. Oh he did, good. I need to know if Gibbs listed any next of kin on his job application. He did? Good, Let me have it. Mother. Winona Gibbs, 5520 East Baltimore Street, Baltimore. Thank you Mr. Jorgason, this information will be a big help. Did he list any references? Okay, good-by."

Next, Jon called Judge Thomas about the search warrant and was told he could come right over.

"Judge, you offered to help bring the mayor's killer to justice."

"I did. What can I do for you?"

"I need a search warrant for the apartment of a man named Backus Gibbs.

"What do you have on Gibbs for probable cause?"

"Here's the affidavit that spells it out, but in summary, we have a security video tape from the mall that

117

shows Gibbs' reflection on the glass of the mall door at the time the mayor came through the door. The image was very weak and we had to have it enhanced. Then we had a police artist make a sketch. The sketch was good enough to locate and identify Gibbs. We have a cigarette butt from the crime scene that we think will have DNA matching his. Also, there is a unique shoe print at the scene that we believe will match one of Gibbs' shoes, if we can find it.

"Detective, all you've got is opportunity, and I can't grant a warrant on that basis. Even if I did, a good lawyer would get it ruled out. You'll have to get me something else, either means, motive, a witness or a confession I'm sorry," he said, and Jon left discouraged.

Sidney Drango was in his office with a drink in his hand, his feet up on the desk and a far away look in his eyes. The small amount of mousy gray hair that he normally combed straight across to cover his baldness was messed up. He had been working on his books assessing where he stood concerning the income from his ten massage parlors, his two adult bookstores, and his part ownership in three strip joints. He estimated that he was on track to achieve his usual six-figure income for the year. The estimate, of course, did not include what he made on drugs, but did include his share of the money laundering for his underworld connections.

He was reflecting that Moreland had been trying to make a name for himself as the cleanup mayor. He was starting early to build a platform for re-election in three years. He hadn't seemed too serious until he forced the Common Council to pass that massage parlor legislation.

Before the legislation had been passed, and while the mayor was making noise, Drango had closed two parlors thinking that it would appease Moreland and slow his efforts. To the contrary, it backfired and seemed to encourage Moreland to get even more aggressive and strict. Drango saw getting rid of Roger Moreland as the only way to save his future in the massage parlor business. He had thought long and hard about how he would eliminate the mayor and decided against putting out a contract on him. The cost was too high and his contacts in the underworld were reluctant to accept the job because of the high visibility such a hit would get.

He felt it was a stroke of genius when he thought about Gibbs. The cost was reasonable and the risk was very low because Gibbs was a nobody and a loner.

Ethan knocked on Drango's office door.

"Who is it?"

"Police, open up!"

The door opened and Ethan said, "Let's go, Drango, we're taking you in for questioning.

"What do you want? What's this all about Williams?"

"Quiet, Drango and let's go."

"I want to call my lawyer."

"What for? I'm not arresting you." He took him by the arm and steered him towards the door. Drango pulled his arm free and said, "You can't make me go and I'm not going."

Ethan said, "Either you go along peaceably or I'll arrest you for suspicion of conspiracy to commit murder.

Which is it going to be?"

"Okay, I'll go but I want my lawyer to be there."

"You can call him when we get there."

Ethan called Jon on his cell phone and told him he was on his way to headquarters with Drango.

Jon called Laurie and told her that he and Ethan were on their way in and would be in the office in about twenty minutes. She said she'd meet them there.

Laurie appeared at Jon's office after Ethan wearing a short black skirt and a white blouse with a black beaded necklace. The outfit, along with her black-rimmed glasses really accentuated her short, curly, black hair.

As she entered the office, Jon said, "This is Laurie Frasier from the DA's office. Laurie, meet Ethan Williams from vice."

"How do you do?" she said, stretching out her hand.

Ethan shook her hand and said, "I've got Drango cooling his heels in interrogation and he's screaming for a lawyer. So why don't we all go down and talk to him."

Standing, Jon said, "The judge turned me down on the search warrant for Gibbs' apartment, didn't think I had enough. How did you make out with the phone records Laurie?"

"They'll be ready for us to pick up at three o'clock." As they were heading out the door, the phone rang and it was Mike. "There's been no action at Gibbs' apartment, so Stern and Pool are staying with the stakeout, and I'm coming into the office for a while." Jon asked him to stop at the phone company on his way in and pick up Gibbs' records for Laurie.

When they entered the ten by twelve foot interrogation room with no windows, Drango was sitting on one of the four straight aluminum framed chairs at the end of the Formica topped table staring at the large mirror on one wall. His hands were interlocked on the table and he started talking as soon as the door was opened. "You guys can't hold me here. I want to see my lawyer now."

"You're not under arrest, what do you want with a lawyer," Ethan asked, stalling for time to make Drango sweat. "We just want to talk to you about Mayor Moreland's murder. We understand that the mayor was squeezing your massage parlor business pretty good. What can you tell us about his death?"

"Nothing, I don't know anything about it. I want my lawyer."

"Here" - Jon threw a notebook and pen on the table - "write down your lawyer's name and phone number and we'll call him for you."

Laurie added, "You know, Drango, I'm from the DA's office and am in a position to make things easier for you if you come clean."

"I don't have anything to say, I didn't do anything."

"We know who did it and we know you're involved. It's just a matter of time until we get the proof we need to arrest you, so why don't you play it smart and come clean. It'll go a lot easier on you if you do".

"I want my lawyer!"

When Mike arrived back at the office, no one else was there, so he sat down and reviewed Gibbs' phone records. There were only fifteen calls and eight were to the same number. He had just gotten off the phone after talking to a supervisor at the phone company. To Laurie, who had just come up from interrogation, he commented, "There are eight calls to a pizza place and three of the others were to Drango's office phone. I think that does it Laurie. We're pretty sure Gibbs did it and these phone records tie him to Drango. Do you think that's enough for us to arrest Drango on suspicion?"

"No. After talking to him, I think we should wait until you pick up Gibbs, and work on him to positively implicate Drango. Like you say, it looks like there is a connection, but if we move too fast and he gets his lawyer involved we might lose him. Now, I'm going down and tell Jon I think we should let him go."

"You guys have done an incredible job to get this far in less than a week."

"We had some good help and some lucky breaks," Mike said, and then added, "It's time for me to go relieve Stern."

Laurie headed back to interrogation and Mike left.

After conferring with Laurie and Ethan outside the interrogation room Jonathan said, "Drango we've decided to let you go, so we didn't call your lawyer. Now get out of here, before I change my mind."

After Drango left, Jonathan, Ethan and Laurie met back at the conference table in the office and Jon remarked, "I found out from the golf course that Gibbs has a mother in Baltimore, and it's my guess that he's on his way there, so I put out an APB with the state police of New York,

Pennsylvania, and Maryland. It's very likely that someone will have to go to Baltimore.

"We may be in luck," Ethan said, "I know a detective in Baltimore pretty well. I'll give her a call and, see if they are willing to help."

"Good, why don't you use Mike's phone, and, Laurie, can you check out extradition considerations with Maryland in case we need I?"

"Sure, may I use your phone?"

"Be my guest."

While the other two were on the desk phones, Jon called Mike on his cell phone. "How's it going?"

"There's been no action at all. I think he's skipped."

"Yeah, I found out he has a mother in Baltimore and I think he might be headed there." Jon told him about the APB's and about Ethan checking with the Baltimore police. Mike, we've been going hard all week, and depending on how Ethan makes out, somebody will probably have to go to Baltimore, so I think we should take a little time to relax this weekend if we can cover everything."

"Yeah, I was talking to Martha about that yesterday and she would like to cook some steaks in the back yard tomorrow. Could you make it if I can work out a schedule with Jay and George on my end?"

"I'll know after Ethan gets off the phone with his contact in Baltimore. Why don't you call me later and we can compare notes and decide."

"I will."

Laurie was off the phone and Jon asked, "How about extradition considerations?"

"No problem, it's not an issue with Maryland, just

requires some paper work which is easy to take care of from either end."

Ethan hung up the phone and turned from the desk saying, "It looks like we're in luck. Elizabeth Jordon, that's the detective I know in Baltimore, has a very light case load right now and thinks she can get her lieutenant to support us for a few days. She's going to call me right back after she checks with him. Beth and I go back a long way. She used to live and work here and we had a thing going for a while. We've talked a few times but haven't seen each other since she left for Baltimore five years ago."

"Here's what I suggest, Jon, I'll leave for Baltimore this afternoon and if I get support from the BPD, you won't have to come down on the weekend. Beth and I will stakeout Gibbs' mother's house and if nothing happens over the weekend you plan to come down either Sunday or Monday, depending on the level of support they provide."

"That sounds great to, me Ethan. Are you sure?"

"Yep, I don't have anything planned for the weekend and I don't mind. To tell you the truth, I'm anxious to see Beth again." The phone rang and it was Elizabeth Jordon offering their support. "I'll go home now, Jon, and call you tonight from Baltimore.

The phone rang again and it was Mike.

Jon filled him in on Ethan's plans. How did you make out on the schedule with Jay and George?"

"They'll cover the apartment tomorrow so I can take a little time in the morning and relieve one of them tomorrow afternoon."

"That's great. Why don't we play nine holes in the morning and then do the steaks? I'll call the captain and fill him in on our plans. I'll get us a tee time at the Greens and let's meet there at ten unless I call you."

CHAPTER FOURTEEN

(*Friday Night*)

On the way to Jessica's, Jonathan stopped at a grocery store and a liquor store. He bought a single red rose bud, a bottle of non-alcoholic chardonnay and a bottle of Glenfidich single malt scotch.

Jonathan drove slowly through the tree lined winding streets of Jessica's upscale condominium development looking for the address that she had given him and was impressed. He saw the number and parked on the street in front of the manicured lawn. When Jessica opened the door, he held out the wine and the rose and said, "Beware of Greeks bearing gifts."

Taking the gifts, she asked, "Are you Greek?"

"No, it was just something to say."

"Well come on in."

"Also," he said, handing her the scotch, "I want you to give this to Frank Salvo. If it's not to his liking, I can take it back and get whatever he likes."

He went into the living room and she went to the kitchen where she put the already chilled bottle of wine in the refrigerator and got a vase of water for the rose. She took the rose to the living room and, setting it on the coffee table, said, "The rose is beautiful, thank you.

"You're welcome."

The living room had a tiled entrance, ivory walls, beige carpeting, and green drapes. The furniture was light green leather nearly the same color as the drapes. Over the mantle was an oil painting of a landscape that also had a lot of green, giving the room an attractive and inviting look.

"Very nice," he said.

"Thanks, how about a drink before we go?"

"It's almost seven thirty, and I made a reservation for eight o'clock. How about a rain check and we'll head right out?"

"Okay," she agreed, starting for the door.

On the way to the restaurant, he said, "I want you to give that bottle of scotch to Frank with my profound thanks because we wouldn't be anywhere without his help."

Inside the restaurant, soft classical music played in the background and there was a candle on every table.

"This is one of my favorite restaurants," Jessica said.

"Good." He smiled, as they sat down.

The waitress brought the menus and asked if they would like something from the bar.

"Give us a couple of minutes with the menu and

then I'll let you know about the drinks."

Jon looked at Jessica and said, "Jess, I don't drink alcohol, so, when I called for the reservation, I asked if they serve non-alcoholic wine and found that they do. So if you don't object, we'll look at the menu and then I'll order a bottle."

"I can live with that," she said.

"What do you think?" he asked, after a few minutes studying the menu.

"I might try the veal."

"And I think I'll try the chicken," so how about a bottle of chardonnay?"

"That sounds good."

The waitress came back and asked," Did you decide?"

"Yes, we'll have a bottle of the Sutter Home non-alcoholic chardonnay, and we'll order after you bring it."

She headed off to get the wine and Jess said, "So let's talk about the Moreland case."

"Jess, I've given some thought about how we should proceed. We have made some progress on the case but I can't give you anything else right now without jeopardizing our investigation. I promise, though, that as soon as it's possible, I'll give you something else and make sure you get it before anyone else."

"You better, she retorted. "If I don't get it first, I'll be in big trouble with my boss and that won't help your cause any."

"I understand, you'll have to trust me."

The waitress was back with the wine. He tasted it and gave her a nod. She filled their glasses and said to Jessica, "Would you like to order now?"

"I'll have the veal piccata, a baked potato with sour cream and butter, and a salad with Thousand Island Dressing."

"And you sir?"

"I'll have the lemon chicken, French fries and salad with crumbly blue cheese dressing."

The waitress was back with the salad and she poured more wine.

Jon lifted his glass in a toast and gave Jessica his best smile.

She toasted back and returned the smile.

"This wine is really good," she said. "I'm not sure I could tell it was non-alcoholic if I didn't know."

"Well it is a varietal wine with the alcohol removed and I think it's pretty good. The bottle I gave you tonight is the same thing, so I'm glad you like it.

During dinner, Jessica said, "Can you tell me why you don't drink alcohol, Jon?"

"For a while after my divorce I was drinking too much. I would go home after work, or stop on the way home, and start drinking, and sometimes would forget about dinner. Quite often I would wake up in the morning, hung-over and feeling awful. One day I realized that I might have a problem, so I talked to Mike about it and he suggested that I go to an AA meeting. At first I felt that wasn't necessary, but the situation didn't improve. In fact, it got worse, because I found myself wanting to drink at lunch and dinner while working and I didn't have the desire or strength to resist. Finally, Mike told me that either I got help or he was going to ask for another partner because there were too many occasions when his ass was dependent on his partner having a clear head. Put to me that way, I relented, knowing that if Mike asked for another partner, I would probably lose my job, since drinking while on the job is strictly prohibited. So I thought about it for a while and finally went to an AA meeting. At first, the meetings were embarrassing and depressing. But after about the fourth meeting, I realized with great clarity, where I was heading if I didn't take action. So I stopped drinking, thinking at the time it would be for a year. That was three years ago and I haven't had a drink since. I feel that I wasn't an alcoholic, but was just feeling sorry for myself because of the divorce and had gotten into a bad habit. Now that I have my life under control, I find that I don't need or miss the alcohol."

"It sounds like you made the right decision," she said. "I can take it or leave it."

After dinner over, dessert and coffee, Jon said, "I'm playing golf in the morning and then going to my partner's house for a steak cookout. How would you like to go to the cookout with me?"

"I can't," she said, "I've got other plans made for tomorrow."

"That's too bad, I'd like for you to meet Mike and his family. Maybe another time. Are you ready to go?"

"Yes, I am."

They were quiet on the way back to Jessica's, both thinking to themselves how much they had enjoyed the evening and wondering if their relationship would blossom.

"You want to come in for that rain check?" she asked.

"I'd love to."

Inside she asked, " What would you like?"

"How about coffee?"

"Coffee it is."

She went to the kitchen, put the coffee on, came back and sat down on the other end of the couch, saying, "I want to thank you for dinner tonight, I really enjoyed it."

"I enjoyed it too. Why haven't we done it before?"

"You never asked."

He had known Jessica for about six years and had always found her attractive, but never thought about asking her for a date. They had met at a crime scene where an enraged and drunk husband had chased his wife out of the house with a knife, chased her around the house and stabbed her just before she reached the porch to go back inside The man was caught about three days later at his girlfriend's on the other side of town. When Jonathan had arrived at the crime scene he found that it hadn't been properly protected and found Jessica and her camera man standing too close to the body. He was furious and read the riot act to Jessica as well as to the police officer whose responsibility it was to protect the scene.

He came out of his reverie and said, "How would you like to play tennis Sunday morning and then go to lunch?"

"I'd like that." What time?" she asked, starting for the kitchen to get the coffee.

"How about nine o'clock?"

"Sounds good," she said, bringing the coffee into the living room and setting the cups on the coffee table. Then she sat down beside him.

After they each had taken a sip, Jon said, "I was thinking about the first time we met. Do you remember?"

"Yes, I do. It took me a while to get over it."

"I was pretty wrapped up in my job at that time, and had just been promoted. I was afraid that if you had messed up that crime scene, it might have major ramifications for my job. It turned out that there was no problem."

"I know now," Jessica said, "that you were right and I was wrong. But I have to tell you that at the time I was really mad."

"I'm glad you're not mad any longer," he said holding his cup up for a toast and adding, "To a future that is more friendly than the past."

"I'll drink to that," she said, as she touched her cup to his and added, "To our future relationship."

He asked, "Are you involved with anyone at this time?"

"No, I was until about three months ago, but it's over. What about you?"

"No, I haven't been involved with anyone seriously since my divorce."

Putting their cups down, Jon turned toward her, took her hand, and asked, "What would you think about dating more so we can get to know each other better?"

"That thought has crossed my mind, and I think we should give it a try and see what happens."

He leaned over and they kissed.

"Would you like more coffee?"

"No, it's late and I'd better go," he said, standing and taking her hand. As she stood, he kissed her again and led her to the door. "I'll pick you up Sunday at nine."

"Ill be ready and waiting," she said, as she opened the door and kissed him good night.

It was six o'clock by the time Ethan got home, packed a bag, and started for Baltimore. The weather was cool and clear. He stopped in Harrisburg for dinner and arrived at the hotel in East Baltimore at eleven, too late to go to the police station, so he called Beth.

"Hi Beth, I just arrived, what's the plan on your end"

"Well, Lieutenant Jones has assigned me to support you full time until next Wednesday unless an emergency arises. Wednesday he wants to take another look at the workload and see where we go from there. He told me to call him at home when you arrived and he would come in and meet with us. Can you be ready by a quarter of twelve?"

"Yeah, I just want to take a fast shower to loosen up the muscles after the trip. According to the map I looked at, the police station isn't far from the place we want to stake out, so I'd like to start the stakeout tonight if it's okay with you."

"Yeah it's okay with me. Tell me where your staying and I'll pick you up."

133

"I'm at the Holiday Inn on O'Donnell just off I 95 in east Baltimore, you know where it is?"

"Yeah, I'll meet you in the lobby at a quarter till twelve."

Ethan took a fast shower and called Jonathan to let him know he had arrived and would start the stakeout right away and call him again tomorrow.

As he entered the lobby, he saw Beth sitting in a chair facing the reception desk. She appeared even more beautiful then he had remembered. Her red curly hair was still long the way he liked it, and she was as shapely as he remembered.

Approaching her, he said, "We should meet like this more often."

She stood and greeted him with a smile and open arms. They hugged and kissed lightly.

"Ready?" she asked.

"Yeah, let's go."

At the station, Beth led the way past the desk sergeant, waving to him as she passed, moving through the bullpen to the lieutenant's office in the back of the room.

"Lieutenant, I want you to meet Ethan Williams from Syracuse."

Chuck Jones was forty, tall, thin, had black wavy hair, and wore gold-rimmed glasses.

Ethan reached out, saying, "Good to meet you Lieutenant and I want to thank you for the help."

"My pleasure," Jones said. You caught us at a good time and Beth was anxious to help you. Besides, this is a high profile case and if we're able to help, it won't hurt my career. Now tell me where you stand."

Ethan briefed him on the facts of the case and confirmed with him that Beth would be able to support him until Wednesday if necessary.

At twelve thirty, Ethan and Beth left to start the stakeout, having agreed on the way to the station that they would take six hour shifts and Beth would go first since Ethan had just driven six hours to get there.

Beth got Winona Gibbs' address from Ethan and dropped him at his hotel.

CHAPTER FIFTEEN

(*Saturday*)

Mike was standing outside the clubhouse when Jon arrived Saturday morning. "Did you get a tee time Jon?"

"Yeah, eight-twelve."

"Good, lets get in line."

"You go first," Mike, said when the tee was clear.

Jon went to the tee with his driver and did a few stretching exercises, put the ball on a tee and addressed it. His swing was nice and smooth and it was a good drive.

"You're going to like that one," Mike said as he came to the tee.

Mike's drive was less spectacular but very playable. Neither got into trouble until number three. Their drives were okay, but the second shot, which has to be played along a very large pond, is where they both got into trouble. Jon put two in the water and Mike three.

On the green, Mike said, " Boy I'm glad this hole is almost behind us. I have never played it without putting at least one ball into the water."

"I did once," Jon said, "but my third shot missed the green, went into the woods, and it took me three to get out. I hate the hole!"

They finished the nine holes and both shot under 50. Not great but not embarrassing either.

"Lets go have some steaks," Mike suggested as they headed for the clubhouse from the ninth green.

"Sounds good to me; let's do it."

"Hi Jimmy," Jonathan said as they walked up the front walk to Mike's house. Jimmy who was sitting in the grass playing with a toy truck, looked up, saw Jon and Mike and yelled, "Hi uncle Jon, hi, Daddy," as he got up and ran towards them.

Jon caught Jimmy as he ran up and gave him a big hug. "How you doing?"

"I'm good," Jimmy said. "Are you staying for steaks Uncle Jon?"

"Sure am."

"That's great. Daddy, can I help with the steaks?"

"Okay, where's your mom?"

"In the house."

Jon and Mike headed for the front door with Jimmy between them.

"We're home Martha, where are you?"

"In the kitchen."

"Are you ready for me to light the grill?" Mike asked, as they entered the kitchen.

She said, "Give me about ten minutes to finish the salad and get the potatoes ready for the microwave. Why don't you and Jon have a drink while you're waiting?" "Hi Jon," she added.

Jon kissed her on the cheek, "Hi, Martha, can we fix you a drink while were at it?"

Thanks, I'll have a glass of white wine, there's a bottle open in the refrigerator."

"What do you want Jon?" Mike asked as he headed for the liquor cabinet.

"Tonic with lime if you have it." He headed to the refrigerator to get the wine for Martha.

Jon set Martha's wine on the counter in front of her and she said, "Why don't you guys go on out in the back yard. Were going to eat at the picnic table and I'll join you there in a few minutes."

Mike and Jon took their drinks and headed for the back yard followed by Jimmy.

"How was the golf?" Martha asked.

"Not great," they said almost in unison. Martha smiled.

"How are things going with the Moreland case?"

"We got a good break with that tape but now we have to find the guy."

"How will you track him down?" she asked.

"Right now we don't have the foggiest," Mike said. "That's a next week problem," and he smiled at her. They had agreed last night that today he and Jon would not talk shop.

"C'mon Tiger," Jon said to Jimmy, "and we'll play ball while your dad gets the grill going."

"Okay, I'll go get the ball," he took off at a run towards the house.

Jon really loved Jimmy, not only because he was a very agreeable and lovable kid, but because he liked kids and never had any of his own. "You bat and I'll pitch Jimmy." After six swings, Jimmy hit the ball and it went about ten yards. Wow," Jon exclaimed, that was a good one. You want to go get it or should I?"

"You go, Uncle Jon, I want to save my strength so I can hit a home run." "Okay Tiger, I'll get it."

"Lets eat." Mike called, as Jon was ready to pitch again. "C'mon Jimmy we'll finish later."

After eating, they sat on the deck and had coffee. Martha said, "Can you believe this weather?"

Mike said to Jon, "How was your date last night?"

"You had a date?" Martha asked in a surprised tone with a smile on her face.

"I had dinner with Jessica Mathews." He smiled.

The Jessica Mathews that's on TV 2?"

"Yeah. It was fine, and we're playing tennis tomorrow."

"Oh?" Mike said. "Sounds like there is some interest."

"I hope it's mutual," Jon said.

Ever since the divorce, Mike and Martha pushed Jon to date more. They would like to see him happily married like they were.

As Jon walked into his apartment, the phone rang. It was Ethan. He told Jonathan about the meeting the night before and that they had been on the stakeout since midnight without any action. "Beth can support us full time until next Wednesday, then her boss will have to take another look at the case load. That means you won't have to come down until at least Tuesday. I'm calling you from my cell phone in the car and I'm parked across the street from Gibbs' mother's house. I've been here since seven and haven't seen any action yet. Beth and I will continue taking six-hour shifts to cover the place around the clock. I'll call you at least once per day or sooner if anything happens."

Beth opened the door, got into the car, and leaned over to give Ethan a kiss. "Hi, any action?"

"No one has gone in or out since I got here. If he's here, he's staying put.

"I'll get in my car and you can go get us some sandwiches while I keep watch. Then when you come back you can keep me company for a while if you're not too tired.

At three o'clock, just as Ethan was getting ready to leave Beth's car, the door of Winona's house opened and a man wearing a blue baseball cap and a blue windbreaker came out. They watched as he headed for the corner. Beth assumed that it was Gibbs and as he turned the corner onto the side street, she started the car, pulled forward a few hundred yards, made a u-turn to come back and turn onto the side street. The man was getting into a car. She pulled up so the car couldn't get out of the parking space and

Ethan jumped out with his gun in hand. "Backus Gibbs? Police, you're under arrest." Gibbs pushed the door of his car towards Ethan and took off around the back of the car. He ran on down the side street and turned right into a narrow alley behind the row houses. Ethan ran after him and Beth pulled out in her car to go around the block, hoping to cut him off at the other end of the alley. Gibbs had a good hundred-yard start on Ethan whose weight slowed him enough to allow Gibbs to widen the gap even further. Gibbs thought about jumping the fence to his mother's back yard and go through her house and across the park. He decided against the move because he didn't want to explain to his mother what was going on. As Gibbs approached the end of the alley he saw Beth's car parked across the entrance and he slowed. He looked over his shoulder and saw Ethan baring down on him from behind, so he picked up speed again and then he saw Beth standing in the middle of the alley entrance in front of her car, feet wide in a stable shooting stance, holding her gun in both hands pointed at him. "Oh no," he said out loud, raising his hands and slowing as he came closer to Beth. He looked over his shoulder again and saw Ethan with gun pulled closing the gap behind him. As Ethan came close, he was out of breath and breathing hard but managed to say, "Backus Gibbs? Police, you're under arrest for the murder of Roger Moreland; put your hands on your head." Gibbs did as he was told and Beth was now along side him with her handcuffs ready, and as she put them on, read him his rights.

"What's this all about?" Gibbs asked, " I didn't do anything."

"C'mon Gibbs, get in the car."

The interrogation room in Baltimore was almost a copy of the one in Syracuse. Maybe a little longer and a little wider and the Formica on the table was green instead of gray. The room had one window with heavy mesh wire over it and the typical large one-way mirror on the wall; Gibbs was sitting at the end of the table with Ethan standing over him.

"You better come clean, Gibbs. You're headed for death row if you don't give us something. We've got proof that you were at the scene. Now tell us why you did it. If somebody else is involved it would be smart for you to tell us. Then we could tell the DA that you cooperated and he might give you a deal."

"What kind of deal?" he asked in a shaky voice."

"Well, maybe you won't get the death penalty. Would you like to live?"

"Yeah, I don't wanta die."

"You should've thought about that before you committed murder."

"I didn't . . ."

"Come on Gibbs," Beth said, "we know you did it, you might as well tell us why and who was in it with you. It'll go a lot easier for you if you talk."

The other detective, Beth's normal partner, Josh Cramer, said, "Why should you take all the blame? All we want is a name and we can get the district attorney to cut you some slack. You'll go to jail for sure, but it could save your life. What do you say?"

Gibbs looked up into the black detective's face and asked, "Would you recommend a minimum sentence if I cooperated?

"Sure", he said. "All three of us would tell the DA how much you cooperated."

"Maybe I should have an attorney, and I want to call my mother."

"Sure, we'll get you an attorney, but when the attorney gets here, you won't be able to say anything and your goose'll be cooked."

"Okay, I did it for Drango."

Gibbs' guilt, residual conscience and the detectives' convincing argument that his case was hopeless had brought the confession and the catharsis that tends to relieve the pain. Gibbs had felt the anguish and pain in an ever increasing manner since the murder, and although it had caused him to flee home to his mother, the pain had not lessened until now when he had actually been able to tell someone that he did it. Confession seems to still the pain and anguish that comes from something like an aching nerve that cannot be precisely located or identified.

"Drango who?" Ethan asked.

"Sidney Drango. I owed him a lot of money and he wanted Moreland dead"

"Why did he want Moreland dead?" Josh probed.

"Moreland was hurting his massage parlor business."

"Will you testify that he hired you?" Ethan asked.

"Yeah."

"Okay, you write it down just the way you told us and sign it." He handed him a pad and a pen. "We'll get you a lawyer when we get back to Syracuse and we'll talk to the district attorney's office and tell them you cooperated."

"Josh." Beth whispered, "You stay with him: make sure he signs an attorney waiver to go with the confession, and take him back to his cell when he's finished. Oh, and let him call his mother. I want to talk to Ethan, and we'll see you back in the office."

"Ethan, it's only Saturday, and the lieutenant said I could support you until Wednesday, so I'll go with you to take him back to Syracuse, if you like, but then I'll have to figure some way to get back home."

"I would like that. Gibbs seems pretty docile right now, but it doesn't pay to take chances. He killed once, so who knows? Syracuse will spring for a rental car for you to get back if that's okay with you."

"Sure, that'd be fine, it's what, a five hour drive?"

"Yeah, a little more or a little less, depending on traffic, weather, and how many times you stop."

"Ethan, the paper work to take him back is pretty simple, so I'll get it ready before I go home today and then we can meet here at seven in the morning, get Gibbs, and head right out.

"Okay, you want to have dinner tonight?"

"Yeah, I'd like that and since you don't know the city, I'll pick you up at seven thirty."

"Great, I'm going back to the hotel and get a couple hours sleep. See you at seven thirty."

"Hi, Mom, it's Backus."
"Where are you, Backus?"

"I'm in jail."

"In jail! What on earth for?"

"I'm in big trouble Mom, I killed a guy."

"What! How could you?"

"Yeah, I'm so sorry now, but it's too late."

"What are you going to do Backus?"

"I gave them a confession Mom. They said it would go easier on me that way. I guess I'll have to go back to Syracuse now."

"Oh Backus, you just came home and now I'm going to lose you again. Can I come see you?"

"I don't know Mom. Let me ask the detective here. Can my mother come see me?"

"Yeah, I guess, tell her to come to the police station on Baltimore Street and tell the desk sergeant what she wants."

Gibbs related the information to his mother and she cried. "I'll come right now, Backus. I love you."

"I love you, too, Mom, and I am sorry."

CHAPTER SIXTEEN

(*Sunday Morning*)

Jon woke Sunday morning to find the sun shining and he smelled coffee. He had put the coffee maker on automatic before he went to bed. He thought, boy that smells good. I should do that every night. But his days were so unpredictable and long that he usually grabbed something on the way home and dropped right into bed as soon as he got there.

Ethan had called him at six o'clock Saturday and told him about the arrest and confession. He, in turn, had called the captain and gave him the good news. Sheppard gave him the okay to inform Jessica of the arrest for the eleven o'clock news Sunday night and said he would call the chief expecting that he would call a press conference for Monday morning. Jon figured, now that they had a confession, he should be able to get Judge Thomas to give him a search warrant. Jon had also called Mike and informed him of the arrest. He directed Mike to continue the stakeout of Gibbs' apartment until he could get the warrant and they could perform a search.

He went to the kitchen and got a cup of coffee, took a sip, then fixed some food for Maggie, who was winding around his ankles as usual. He took the coffee to the bathroom with him and after showering and shaving, went back to the kitchen to get some breakfast and call Judge Thomas at home to inform him of the arrest and confession. he made an appointment for two o'clock at the judge's home to get the search warrant signed.

Jon knocked on Jessica's door at five minutes after nine. When she opened the door, she was dressed in white shorts and a white knit top. She looked ravishing and he told her so.

"Why, thank you kind sir," she said, as she held the door open for him to come in.

"Are you ready to go?" he asked, while still standing in the entrance to the living room.

"Yes."

"Okay lets go. I thought we would play an outside court over near where I live if it's ok with you."

"It is," she said, as they turned toward the door. It took about a half hour to get to the tennis courts located three blocks from the golf course clubhouse. The courts were empty when they arrived and the sun was still shining. The temperature was supposed to reach sixty degrees. That was very unusual for early November, but was perfect for tennis and very welcome after the snow and freezing rain they'd had on Thursday.

On the court, Jonathan said, "You wanta volley for the serve?"

"Okay."

Jon bounced the ball on the court once and lobbed it over the net to her. She returned it and he spiked it down towards her feet and she missed it.

"So that's the way you're going to play, huh?"

"My serve." He smiled.

His first two serves hit the net. The third serve was good and Jessica returned it with a vengeance, and so it went. Jessica won one game and Jonathan two. They discussed playing another set but decided against it because the temperature had, in fact, reached the high sixties and the humidity was high. Even though it was now overcast, they were hot. Coming off the court, Jonathan said, "Let's go to the Greens clubhouse for lunch; it's close and it's air-conditioned."

"Sounds good." She puffed, as she put her racket and three balls into a bag. They got into the truck and drove the short distance to the clubhouse.

When they entered the bar of the restaurant, the air-conditioning felt wonderful. The bar was rather dark and empty, so they decided to go straight into the restaurant.

The waitress who came to wait on them was a tall girl with short bobbed blond hair and a chubby face.

"Would you like something from the bar?"

"I'd like a wine cooler."

"And you sir?"

"I'll have a coke."

As the waitress turned away, Jessica remarked, "I don't think you were very nice during the game."

"Why?" he asked.

"Don't you think you were kind of aggressive?"

"That's the way I play, you didn't want me to just let you win, did you?"

"No, but you could have been a little less aggressive."

"Okay, I'll try harder next time to be nicer."

"Good."

The waitress came and they both ordered hamburgers and French fries.

"Jon where are you with the investigation?"

"I've got some good news for you Jess. We arrested the murderer in Baltimore last night and he's being brought back today. I got approval from the captain for you to use the information on the eleven o'clock news tonight. There will probably be a news conference Monday morning to make it public, though I don't have conformation on that yet. The guy's being brought back to Syracuse as we speak. I don't want you to say any more than what I just told you because we still have some follow up work to do and I don't want that jeopardized.

Back at Jessica's condo, she asked, "Would you like to come in for a drink?"

"Thanks, but I can't. I've got an appointment related to the case at two that I have to keep. You're not mad at me about the tennis?"

"No, of course not. The next time we play, I'll get even, now that I know how dirty you play."

"You wanta bet?"

"We'll see," she said, as they walked up to the door.

"You know Jon, I really enjoyed myself Friday night and today."

"I did too, and hope we can do a lot more of it. What do you think?"

"Okay, if you insist. How about dinner tonight here, and let me demonstrate my extensive culinary skills?"

"You've got it, my mother taught me that the way to a man's heart is through his stomach, so tonight's your chance."

She laughed and kissed him.

He looked at his watch and said, " If I'm going to make my appointment and dinner date, I'd better go home and get cleaned up. What time do you want me back?"

"Actually, I don't want you to go," she said, "but if you must, how about being back at seven thirty?"

Jonathan brushed and fed Maggie when he got home and then went for a short walk before getting into the shower.

He had just finished dressing in gray slacks, a pale blue button down shirt and a navy blazer when Ethan called, telling him that they were back in Syracuse and had Gibbs locked up. Jonathan informed him that he was about to leave for an appointment with the judge to get a search warrant for Gibbs' apartment and asked Ethan to meet him in the office at four o'clock.

Jon waited inside the judge's front door while the judge looked at the search warrant. "You understand

Detective that this warrant will cover only the suspect's apartment and his place of work." He signed the three copies and handed two of them back to Jon.

"Thanks Judge."

As Jon walked up to the car, Mike rolled down the window. "Has anything happened Mike?"

"Things have been quiet. Did you get the warrant?"

"Yeah, let's go."

As Mike followed Jon across the street, he told him that the apartment house manager lived in the basement apartment and they headed for that door. When Jon knocked on the door, he heard a muffled voice yell, "Just a minute." The door opened suddenly to reveal a gray, frizzy haired man in his early fifties. He was overweight, in a tee shirt and was smoking a cigar. "Yeah?" He mumbled through his teeth and around the cigar.

"We're the police and have a search warrant for Gibbs' apartment. Since we have him in jail, we need you to open the apartment.

"What did he do?"

"Can't say right now, let's go."

You sure this is legal and I won't get into any kind of trouble?"

"Yeah," Jon waived the search warrant, saying, "This makes it legal." They followed the manager up the steps and waited while he knocked on the door and then opened it. As they stepped inside, Jon said to the manager, "You can go now, we'll leave a list of anything we take and a copy of the search warrant where they can be easily found. Thank you."

After the manager left, they turned on the light and Jon motioned, motioning the other side of the room, said, "You take that side and I'll take this side."

"Not much of an apartment," Mike commented, as he turned left and headed for a set of bookshelves. Jon opened a closet door in the corner near the door. It contained an assortment of shirts, pants, jackets and coats. On the floor, he noticed a green and yellow plastic box with a hasp catch. He pulled it out and opened it. "I'll be a son-of-a-bitch!" he exclaimed.

"What is it?" Mike asked.

"A fishing knife, and about the right size. What do you bet it has Moreland's blood on it?" Jon pulled a plastic bag from his pocket and without touching the knife, manipulated it into the bag. He didn't find anything else of importance in the closet and turned to the drawers of a dresser against the wall. He went through each drawer starting, with the bottom one, and didn't find anything until he got to the middle drawer of three drawers across the top. In the bottom of the drawer under a bunch of socks, was a leather-covered blackjack. "Well, well, lookie here."

"What?"

"A blackjack, and probably the murder weapon."

Mike called out, "Look at this." He had just finished going through a drawer in a table beside a chair. He held up a stack of papers. "These are IOUs made out to Sidney Drango and signed by Gibbs. There sure is a bunch of them."

"I'll be," Jon said. "Well, that corroborates what Gibbs told Ethan. I think that's it. I don't see any place else to search. He scribbled out a receipt for the knife,

152

blackjack and vouchers and left it with a copy of the search warrant on top of the dresser. On the way out, he remarked, "you know, we didn't find any shoes. I wonder if he has a locker at the golf course where he works? Mike, here's another copy of the search warrant, I'll take this evidence in and get it logged, and you run out to the golf course and check for a locker."

Before Jon started back to the office, he called Ethan and Laurie Frasier and asked them to meet him there.

Laurie appeared at Jon's office before Ethan and, as she entered the office, Jon pointed, saying "Here comes Ethan right behind you." Then so both could hear he added, "The search of Gibbs' apartment turned up a knife, a blackjack, and IOUs signed by Gibbs and made out to Drango. I'd say that about wraps it up. We already have the phone connection between Gibbs and Drango. The only other things that might help is a DNA match on the cigarette butt found at the scene and a pair of shoes with a crescent shaped chunk out of the sole to match the print at the scene. Mike is on his way out to the golf course where Gibbs works to see if there is a locker containing shoes. Good chance, I'd say, since grass cutting is a messy job. I'll talk to the judge later about a court order for a blood sample if Gibbs refuses to give us one."

Ethan said, "This is Detective Beth Jordon with the Baltimore police," pointing over his shoulder to the tall thin redhead with a pug nose and green eyes wearing a blue pant suit.

After introductions, Ethan said, " From what I just heard, Jon, I think we can go arrest Drango."

"I agree," Laurie said. "Ethan, why don't you and Beth do that and Jon and I can go talk to Gibbs about the blood sample. When we all get back here, maybe Mike will be back with the results of his search at the golf course."

To the man at the counter in the pro shop, Mike said, "I'd like to speak with Chris Jorgason, the pro. Do you know where he is?"

"Try the building out by the parking lot. He's usually there in his office when he's not giving a lesson. If he's not there, try the driving range which is down there." He pointed towards a sloping bank to the left of the clubhouse.

"Thanks."

Mike walked across the parking lot and into the maintenance building saying to the man at a desk with his back to him, "Chris Jorgason?"

"Yeah?"

Mike showed his badge and said, "I'm Detective Crane with the Syracuse police. Does Backus Gibbs have a locker or some place where he keeps personal stuff while he's working."

"Yeah, he has a locker. It's on the other side of the building. C'mon and I'll show you. What's he done?"

"Can't tell you."

"Are you looking for anything in particular Detective?"

"Yeah, a pair of shoes."

"Here's his locker, it's not locked, so help yourself. Oh, by the way, do you have a search warrant?"

"Yeah," Mike said, as he pulled the warrant out and waved it. He opened the locker. There, sitting on the bottom of the locker was a pair of old grass-stained sneakers. He picked them up and looked at the bottoms. "Bingo!" he cried, "Here it is." On the bottom of one of the sneakers was a gouged out area shaped like a crescent. "That's what I was looking for," he said, as he pointed to the gouge in the sole. He pulled out a plastic bag, dropped the sneakers into it, thanked Jorgason, and headed for his car.

CHAPTER SEVENTEEN

(*Sunday Afternoon*)

Ethan and Beth knocked on Drango's office door several times and got no answer. Ethan said, "Let's try the massage parlor. It's just down there at the end of the mall." They decided to drive the short distance rather than walk so they would be closer to the car when they arrested Drango. The Strip mall had seen better days. There were provisions for about ten stores and most of them were empty. There was a drugstore and cleaner still open plus the massage parlor. The window and door of the massage parlor were covered with opaque curtains giving the appearance that the place was closed, but the outside was brightly lighted with a red neon sign over the door reading 'ECSTASY'. In the window, there was a poster sign.

'FULL BODY RUBS
PERSONAL ATTENTION
TO EVERY DETAIL'

They opened the door and went in. There was as skinny man at the counter with black slicked down hair.

"Can I help you?"

Ethan showed his badge and said, "We're looking for Sidney Drango."

"He ain't here."

"Where can we find him?"

"How would I know?"

"You work for him, don't you?"

"Yeah, but he only comes in Saturdays to collect the money, and I don't know where he hangs out. Try his office down the street;" he pointed in the direction from which they had just come.

"Was he here yesterday?"

"Yeah."

"What time?"

"About six."

Did he say anything about where he was going?"

"Not to me."

"Let's go Beth.

Outside, Ethan said, "Let's try his house. He lives about a half hour east of here."

"You seem pretty familiar with this guy."

"Yeah, I've been keeping a loose watch on him for a couple of years, he's involved in all kinds of stuff, but we haven't been able to catch him in the act on anything worth while."

Drango's house was located at the end of a long dead end street. It was a big two-story brick sitting back from the road on a very large lot. As they drove in the circular driveway, Beth said, "Quite a view," as she looked past the house at the large lake in the distance.

"Yeah, all it takes is money, and this two bit crook has plenty."

The place seemed deserted as they approached the door. They rang the bell several times and there was no answer.

On the way back to the office Ethan said to Beth, "I think we should put a stakeout on his office, parlor, and house. The office and massage parlor will be easy, but the house presents a bit of a problem. A car parked on that street would really stand out. Even regular drives past would probably be noticed."

"Beth said, "What about a county or town sewer detail?"

"That might work, but better then sewers would be cable TV or telephone. All of these neighborhoods have underground service. I'd have to make special arrangements, which shouldn't be too much of a problem. We could set up a barricade around an access box and park a van on the street. We could use a cover story that we have almost a hundred families between Manlius and Fayetteville with either bad TV reception or no reception at all. Do you know how irate customers get when their TV's don't work?" He smiled. "We've got to work around the clock to get it fixed. The street where were working is at a major juncture with the other locations."

When Ethan and Beth arrived back at the office, Jon, Mike and Laurie were already there. After introducing Beth to Mike, Ethan said, "We couldn't find Drango at his office, the Ecstasy parlor or his house. He has a lot of other interests and could be anywhere. I think we should put a stakeout on those three locations. He's very likely to show up at one of them soon."

Jon said to Laurie, "We've got Gibbs' confession, the knife, the blackjack, the IOUs, and the phone records. Do you think that's enough for the grand jury to indict Drango as well as Gibbs?"

"I think so. And in Gibbs' case I think I'll wait for the crime lab and the coroner to check the blackjack for Moreland's hair and the knife for his blood. We'll also use the blood sample we just got from Gibbs to check the cigarette butt. But I don't feel that I need that result to go to the grand jury. I should be able to take both cases to them by the middle of the week. We can arrest Drango before or after that, it doesn't matter."

Ethan said, "Who has a good contact at the TV Cable Company?"

"I know a manager in the downtown office. Laurie said, "Why?"

"We need to borrow a truck, about three pair of coveralls and some barricade paraphernalia to set up the stakeout on Drango's house which is on a quiet residential street. That's about the only way we can do it without raising suspicion. Do you think you can swing it and make it happen this afternoon?"

"It's almost five, let me call him right now."

While Laurie was making the call, Ethan said to

159

Mike, can you, Jay, and George handle the stakeout on Drango's office and the Ecstasy Parlor if Beth and I handle his house?"

"Sure, You give me the addresses and I'll call them on my way over there. They're waiting to hear from me for their next move." Rising to leave, Ethan handed him a slip of paper containing the location of the office and massage parlor.

Laurie hung up and said, "Pete Ford, the cable TV manager, says he can help us and wants you to come to their office at 403 Clinton Street right away. They close at six."

Ethan jotted down the address and said, "Let's go, Beth."

Jon was left alone in the office and sat for a few minutes thinking, as soon as they arrested Drango, it would be over. He updated the board and went home to get ready for his seven-thirty dinner date with Jessica. He could hardly wait and was glad that Ethan and Mike were covering the Drango bases. Before he left, he called them to make sure everything was going according to plan. Just as he was ready to leave, the captain called and told him to meet them downstairs in front of the building at eight the next morning for a news conference.

When he got home, Jon decided that he had time for a walk that he felt would relax him. He brushed and fed Maggie and put on a pot of coffee before heading out on the path that would circle Oberon Lake and loop back to his apartment in about twenty minutes. He liked walking around the pond where he usually saw mallards, Canada geese and sometimes a blue heron.

After the walk and a cup of coffee, he felt great. The case was rapidly coming to a close and he could have dinner with Jessica and not worry about the job. At seven o'clock, he finished dressing and headed out for Jessica's.

"Perfect timing Jon, c'mon in. For dinner I've prepared lamb chops with mint jelly, squash, green beans and a salad. For wine I have a non-alcoholic Cabernet Sauvignon, which you can open and pour while I finish the salad. The wine is at room temperature. I hope that's okay with you."

"Perfect, just the way I like it." He followed her to the kitchen and poured the wine while she placed the food on the table. "I'd say we make a pretty good team."

"I noticed that," she said as Jon set the wine glasses at their places. They sat down in the candlelight with the CD playing Mantovani softly in the background.

He held his glass out for a toast, and the glasses clinked. After he had taken the first bite of lamb, he said, "Mmm, did I tell you that lamb is one of my favorites?"

"No you didn't, I fixed it because it's one of my favorites also."

"One of these days," he said, "I'll take you to a little Lebanese restaurant I know about an hour's drive from here that serves really great lamb, almost as good as this." He smiled.

After they had finished dessert and coffee, Jon turned on the TV and they watched Jessica's taped report

161

on the Moreland case arrest. Afterward, rising from the couch, he said, "I think I should go". He held out his hand to help her up and they walked to the door and kissed good night.

CHAPTER EIGHTEEN

(*Sunday Night*)

The Scossi property sat way back from the road with an eight-foot wrought iron fence around it. By some standards, it would be considered a mansion with its fifteen rooms and eight baths. It had a commanding view of the lake and was only partially lighted.

It was a cold evening and Tony Scossi had a fire going in the gas fireplace in his billiards room. Tony and Sid Drango were playing pool. Drango made the five-ball in the corner pocket, rose, and said, "I didn't like the sounds of that news conference Friday morning, the cops claiming to have a clue that will lead to Gibbs' arrest. I'm worried because if they do catch that little creep and squeeze him, I know he'll talk. Of course maybe they're just blowing smoke and don't have shit."

CLYDE SKAGGS

"Walking away from the fire where he had been leaning against the mantle with his drink, Tony walked towards the pool table and around to the other side to take his shot. Leaning over the table, he said, I told you six months ago when you asked about putting out a contract on Moreland that it was a bad idea. And it was even dumber to hire an amateur like Gibbs, because amateurs almost always get caught and you can't rely on them to keep their mouths shut. Sid, if I were you, I'd think about getting out of town until you see which way the wind blows. If you're interested, I've got a good friend in St Martin that would give you a place to stay for a while and that's far enough off the beaten track that you should be safe. This isn't a bad time to think about going south either, because the damn weather's already starting to get iffy. Boy, I hate the cold weather."

"What would I do about the business, Tony? I've got weekly collections to make and I've got your money that has to be funneled through the operations, and I don't have anybody that I trust to handle those things."

"Well if you decide you should go, I can keep things going for you on this end. I've got some good people working for me that I trust. All you have to do is fill me in on what needs to be done."

"What's St. Martin like? I've never been there."

"Man, you'd love it. The temperature's eighty degrees year round and they've got nude beaches on the French side where you can go and watch the naked girls. Also they drive on the right side of the road and use the American dollar as standard currency. It's almost like being home, only it's warm. All the time."

164

"Do you think I should go, Tony?"

Before he could answer, Tony pointed at the TV with the hand holding his drink, and yelled, "Listen!" The eleven o'clock news had just come on and Jessica Mathews was giving a special report. " . . . was learned that yesterday in Baltimore, Maryland, a man was arrested for the murder of Roger Moreland. He is now in the Syracuse jail. There are no details available at this . . ." Tony switched the TV off and turning towards Drango said, "Sid, I think you're in big trouble. If they arrested that guy yesterday, there's a good chance that he's already squealed. If I were you, I wouldn't even go home. I'd just get out of Syracuse. It'd be my guess that, if Gibbs talked, they're watching your house and your office."

"Shit, Tell me about your contact in St. Martin."

"Her name is Lilly Wilhelm, she owns an adult bookstore and lives on the Dutch side of the island in Upper Princes Quarter. I'll call her right now."

"As he used his cell phone to dial, Drango noticed that he didn't have to look up the number.

"Lilly this is Tony."

"Hi Tony, long time no hear, what's up?"

"Lilly, I've got a friend here with me that's in some trouble. We think the cops may be laying for him at his office and his house. I think he should get out of the country tonight if possible. Could you put him up for a while till he finds out what's going on? I know it's pretty short notice and I'd understand if you can't do it."

"Don't worry Tony, it's not a problem, I'll work it out. There's a plane that comes in here every morning from New York. Gets here between ten and eleven. If your

165

friend can get to New York tonight, he should be able to get that plane in the morning if it's not full. You better tell him to get a reservation right away and don't wait until tomorrow, because the plane is usually loaded. If it's as serious as you say, I think he should go to New York tonight whether he gets on that morning flight or not. He'll probably be safer in New York then where he is if he can't go home."

Lil was talking from experience because she had been in similar situations more than once and knew that it didn't pay to hesitate.

"What's his name?"

"Sidney Drango."

"Okay, give him my number and tell him I'll plan to pick him up at the St Martin airport tomorrow morning unless I hear from him. If he doesn't get on that early flight tomorrow, tell him to call me and let me know what his plans are. What's he look like?"

"He's short, fat and starting to go bald."

"Okay Tony, I'll take care of him for you."

"Thanks Lil, I owe you."

After he hung up, Drango said, "Gee, thanks, Tony, for that glowing description you gave her."

"Don't blame me, I've been telling you for two years you should lose weight." Now tell me what I need to do for you while you're gone."

"Okay. I've got the ten massage parlors where the money has to be picked up every Saturday. I've got the two bookstores where I pick up the receipts on Mondays. The three strip joints aren't as big a problem. Somebody else picks up the money there so you don't have to worry about that. The bookkeeper works the laundering deal and interfaces directly with me on that, so I'll give you his name and I suggest you interface with him personally. I'll also give you the addresses of the parlors and bookstores so you can make the pickups. Would you do me a favor, Tony, and call the airport and see if you can get me a reservation to St. Martin while I write down this information for you?"

Seeing how nervous his friend was Scossi said, "Sure Sid, I can do that. Do you care where you stay in New York?"

"No, just make it at the airport so it's convenient"

"How 'bout a drink before I make the call?"

"Yeah, scotch on the rocks. Make it a double, I really need a drink."

After preparing the drinks, Tony sat down in an overstuffed chair by the fire and used his cell phone again to call the airport. He got Sid on the one-fifteen USAir flight to Kennedy, a reservation on an American flight to St Martin at six thirty in the morning and booked him into the Holiday Inn at Kennedy. After he hung up, he told Sid about the reservations he'd made, and the two of them went over the list of information that Drango had prepared while he was on the phone. Then, Drango said, "I'm going past the office on the way to the airport to get some cash and my passport. I'm afraid to leave the country without a passport. I won't worry about clothes, I can buy some when I get to St. Martin."

"You'd better get going Sid, You've only got about an hour and an half to catch the plane."

Jay and George were parked near four other cars in

167

the parking lot where they would not be noticed and where they could see both the massage parlor and Drango's office. They had been there about six hours and were due to be relieved by Mike at any minute when Jay saw someone pull up in front of Drango's office and park. "Looks like some action," he said to George.

George looked around and started the car, saying, "I'll let him get inside and then drive over."

He pulled up along side the building a short ways from Drango's door and they got out of the car. Jay walked up to one side of the door and George to the other side. They both pulled their guns and waited.

When Drango came rushing out, George moved between him and the door and said, "Drango, put your hands on your head, you're under arrest for conspiracy to commit murder."

"Oh bull." "Drango said, then added, "You don't have anything on me, I wanta see my lawyer."

Jay rushed up and put the handcuffs on him while George read him his rights.

On their way to the station with Drango, George called Mike, Jonathan, and Ethan to give them the good news. They agreed to all meet in Jonathan's office.

Jonathan met with the other detectives in the office, and to Beth he said, "Tell your boss if he ever needs help in the Syracuse area to be sure and give me a call. And Beth, thank you very much for your help. When you're ready to go back to Baltimore, rent a car and send me the bill so I can get you reimbursed." To Ethan, Jay, and George he said, "The captain will call each of your bosses and thank them personally for your help." He stood and shook everybody's hand before they left. And to Mike, "I'll see you in the morning Partner."

After everyone left, he called Captain Sheppard and gave him the good news. "Captain, if it's okay with you, I'd like to call Jessica Mathews and give her the wrap up information."

"No problem Jon, but ask her to wait an hour to release the information so I can call the chief. And thanks, Jon, for a job well done."

Jon pressed the button on the phone and dialed again. "Hi Jess sorry to call you so late, but I wanted to let you know we made a second arrest in the Moreland case which wraps it up. Backus Gibbs, the guy we arrested in Baltimore says he was hired by a massage parlor owner named Sidney Drango who was arrested and booked a few minutes ago. The district attorney's office will be going to the grand jury for indictments on both suspects by the middle of the week."

"That's wonderful Jon, The manager will want to air a special bulletin right away. Is it okay?"

"Yeah, the captain asked that you wait an hour so he can inform the chief. Oh, and Jess, remember that they're innocent until proven guilty, so use the word suspect liberally in your report."

"Sure, I always do. Jon, I know its late but how would you like to come over for a midnight snack?"

"Hi," Jessica said, as she opened the door.

Jon said, "Hi," and added, "Boy, it's been a long day."

169

"Come on in. What would you like to eat? I've got a pizza in the freezer, or I could make a salad with chicken, or scrambled eggs."

"Salad sounds good."

"Salad it is. Would you like some olives and peperincini in it?"

"Sounds great."

"How about some coffee?" Jon asked.

"Great, why don't you do that while I work on the salad?"

As he was filling the pot, Jessica set the coffee on the counter beside him and started to break the lettuce into a large salad bowl. After the coffee was started, Jon came up behind her, put his arms around her, and kissed her on the neck and ear.

"We may never eat if you don't stop."

"Killjoy."

"Not kill, postpone. It's late and I still have to go to the station. So we better work on eating first."

"Okay," he said, opening the cabinet and removing two cups. As he poured the coffee and she put the dressing on the salad, she asked, is there anything else you can tell me?"

"No, the case is closed as far as I'm concerned. The rest is up to the DA."

After eating, they moved to the couch for a while before Jessica had to leave for the station and Jon had to go home and feed Maggie.

After they kissed at the front door, Jon said, "I'll call you sometime tomorrow."

Outside, he said, "Thanks for the snack."

"You're welcome, and I'll be waiting for your call tomorrow." They kissed again and she headed for her car and he for his truck.

(Monday Morning)

As Jon approached the front of Police headquarters, he had to force his way through the crowd of reporters. Mike, Captain Sheppard and Chief Webster were already there. Jon approached and greeted them as Webster walked up to the microphone. He noticed the chief had on his gray pinstripe suit, a white shirt, and red tie. He looked quite dashing as he placed his hands on the portable podium and said, "Thank you for coming ladies and gentlemen. It gives me great pleasure to report this morning that we have arrested two suspects in the Roger Moreland murder case. The man arrested for the actual murder is Backus Gibbs and that arrest was made in Baltimore, Maryland with the cooperation of the police there. The investigation continued after that arrest and another suspect by the name of Sidney Drango was arrested late last night on conspiracy charges. The case is considered closed from the police standpoint and the district attorney plans to go to the grand jury for indictments by the middle of the week. I want to publicly commend the detectives who worked on this case day and night to bring it to a close in a very short five days. Also a special thanks goes to the Baltimore police for their help. Specifically I want to recognize Lieutenant Josh Jones and the detective whom he assigned, Detective Beth Jordon. I thank you again for coming." The news conference was over and they entered the building without taking any questions.

Jon and Mike went to the office and made a pot of coffee. While waiting for it to brew, Jon said, "It really feels good to be done with this case."

"I agree," Mike said, and on the way back to their desks, added, "Should I erase the board?"

"Yeah, it's time to start fresh. We shouldn't need that stuff any more and, if we do, it's documented in our reports and notebooks. While Mike was erasing the board, Jon sat down at his desk with his coffee and called Jess.

"Good morning, this is the call I promised. How would you like to go to dinner tonight and celebrate?

"I'd love to, what time?"

"How about eight o'clock and we'll do Italian?"

"I'll be waiting".